SWAGMAN

THE GUARDIANS OF TIME ⏱ BOOK ONE

SWAGMAN

THE GUARDIANS OF TIME ◉ BOOK ONE

VIVIENNE LEE FRASER

www.viviennelfraser.com.au

First published in Australia 2019 by Vivienne Lee Fraser

The right of Vivienne Lee Fraser to be identified as the author of this work has been

asserted by her under the *Copyright Amendment (Moral Rights) Act 2000.*

This is a work of fiction. Names, characters, businesses, places, events and incidents are either the products of the author's imagination or used in a fictitious manner. Any resemblance to actual persons living or dead, or actual events, is purely coincidental.

Vivienne Lee Fraser
www.viviennelfraser.com.au

Cataloguing-in-Publication details are available
from the National Library of Australia
www.trove.nla.gov.au
ISBN: 978-0-6482181-7-3

Formatting and cover design by KILA Designs
www.kiladesigns.com.au
Cover images: © bigstockphoto.com | depositphotos.com

This book will always be for my dad.
Although he will never read it, I owe its inspiration
to him, and I hope it would bring a smile to his face.

PROLOGUE

Early autumn sunlight dappled the forest floor as beating hooves sent the woodland animals scurrying for cover. Sounds of horses crashing through the undergrowth filled the air as the disturbance drew closer. The man glanced around, desperately searching for somewhere safe to hide. These forests were reserved for the royal hunt and, while no edicts had been issued to prevent the collection of wood from crown lands, no one had given him permission to gather there either.

Spying a clump of bushes close to a large tree, the man dragged his load over and hid himself, hoping the shelter would keep him safe from prying eyes and trampling feet. He took his place not a minute too soon. A stag crashed through the foliage, stopping abruptly in the clearing. Ears pricked, the animal stood quivering with exertion, listening for his pursuers.

For a second the woods fell silent. Droplets of blood

dripped to the ground from a flesh wound on the deer's flank. The man knew the king and his cronies would not allow this creature to live. He surveyed the bushes. The slight movement of a branch here, and a crackle of leaves there, telling him men were moving into position to surround the injured beast.

Eyes swung in fear as the deer realised too late it was trapped. Stamping, nervously seeking a way through the ring of men, its eyes found his. When recounting his tale later, he would swear the poor animal begged him for his life.

From his hiding place, the man observed the hunters reveal themselves. One by one they emerged from the undergrowth, standing silently, until the eerie quiet was disturbed by the twang of a bow string. A lone arrow sped through the air. At the last moment, the frightened beast stepped aside and the bolt whizzed past, finding its home in the stomach of the man standing opposite.

The corpulent target fell to the ground, and time stood still as the watching men collectively gasped. The thud when the body hit the forest floor broke the spell, spurring a frenzy of action. Forgotten, the deer made the most of the distraction and slipped quietly away, while frantic men rushed to their dying comrade. First to reach him, the bowman dropped to his knees beside the body.

'Sire. Sire, what have I done?' He wrenched the offending arrow from the prone figure.

As the other hunters drew forward, the injured man clutched at his stomach, as if to halt the flow of blood. Body shuddering, his arms fell to the ground and his eyes stared sightlessly at the canopy of leaves above.

SWAGMAN

'Tirel, you fool, you should have left well alone. Gut wounds are always tricky,' one of the hunters shouted as he reached the group. 'Here, let me look at him. My god, man, you killed the king.'

'But … but … you all saw I shot at the stag. It was an accident,' the stricken bowman wailed.

'We know, but others may not see it that way. Best you get away from here. Head to your lands in Normandie until we sort things out. Go on, quickly, before the rest of them catch us up.'

The pale killer tripped and stumbled in a daze as he left his fellow huntsmen. Seconds later, the sound of retreating hoofbeats confirmed he fled from the scene of his crime as instructed.

Realising he would not now be able to move until the hunters left, the silent witness settled in to observe the historic event unfold in front of him. Not knowing what to do, the men stood staring at each other, as if waiting for someone else to take control. More horses burst into the clearing. A dark haired, wiry man in royal purple dismounted and strode over to the body, whose lifeforce now mingled with the blood of the deer he had chased to his own death.

'The New Forest has claimed another of my brothers. Well, the monk did warn King William if he hunted today, he would not return home. The fool should have listened. Come, our king is dead. There is much to do. When we reach the others, we will send a servant back to bring the body home.'

Leaving the dead king, the nobles of the land abandoned their monarch as if he were no more to them than the animals they chased and killed for sport. They made haste back to Winchester to begin their plotting and planning.

Once the woods were again free of the sound of hunters and horses, the elderly man rose, stretched out the creaks in his body, and walked over to the ruler of Briton. Though he tried, he could not summon pity for the dead man's fate. He had not been a good king. He had not been well liked. Even so, he did not deserve to end his days rotting in the forest, waiting for servants to come find him.

He retraced his steps until he reached his donkey and cart. After a short walk back to the forest glade, he threw the logs from his hiding place into the cart, where they clattered on top of those he had already collected that day. He moved them around to make a bed for King William Rufus' body. As a charcoal burner, he could not afford to lose any of his haul, even if his cart was to carry a king.

Making sure everything was secure, the man set off to find the servants from Winchester Castle. The woodsmen knew him and they would be pleased he saved them the effort of collecting the body, most likely even pay him a little something for his efforts.

In his bones he understood he was witness to a pivotal point in the history of this land. He decided once the body was delivered and the reward collected, he would find the apothecary Master Gavin. Together they might be able to do something to ensure the light shone more brightly in Briton after these dark days.

CHAPTER ONE
ONCE A JOLLY SWAGMAN

John stopped dead in the middle of the street as men, boys and a smattering of women continued to swarm around him, faces fierce and determined. As hundreds of feet kicked up dust, and hundreds of voices yelled and screamed and demanded attention, he wondered how the peaceful protest had so quickly turned into a full scale riot.

Turning at the sound of breaking glass, he spotted a group cheering as the window of a farm goods store cracked, then shattered to the ground. Spurred on by the violent act, others picked up stones and began pelting buildings along Main Street, uncaring whether the owners supported the landholders or them.

One storekeeper was foolish enough to come out to protect his property, but swayed and nearly fell as a stray rock opened a bloody gash on his cheek. John went to go forward and help, after all the man was one of the few in town who offered work to striking shearers from the camp, but the store keeper rushed back inside, firmly bolting the door.

Making his way back through the angry crowd, he marvelled how the men moved to let him past, like a river flowing around a rock. As the mob finally began to thin, he came upon a group of boys around his own age, surrounding a young girl and her mother, they were jeering and yelling insults. The woman held her daughter in the protective circle of her arms, staring defiantly at their attackers, her trembling hands the only indication of her fear.

Blue eyes found his, and his anger was ignited by the plea she sent him. These boys must have mothers and sisters of their own. How would they feel if someone treated them this way? Besides, their argument was with the landholders and the wealthy townsmen who supported the cutting of shearer's wages, not women like this. Women had no more say in pay rates and working conditions than the men themselves did. In fact, many would argue they had even less.

Pushing his way through the group, he found the woman's hand and prepared to lead her away. Before he could, the circle closed back around them, voicing their protests at his interference.

'Hey, what are you doing?'

'You are meant to be on our side.'

'Class traitor.'

John glared at them, saying nothing but defying them

SWAGMAN

to take him on. Something in his look caused the aggressors to pause, and he took the opportunity to break free, dragging the woman and her daughter behind him.

Slipping between two buildings, he led them through to a back street. It was deserted and seemed eerily quiet after the noise the striking shearers made. As he checked they had not been followed, the woman touched his arm and smiled gratefully at him.

'Thank you. Goodness knows what those boys would have done.'

'It was nothing,' John mumbled. 'I hope someone would do the same for my mam and sister. They would not have hurt you—I don't think they would have any way. They are just angry, and perhaps hungry too. They got carried away.

'If you head home through the back streets you should be safe enough, but lock your door when you get there, just to be sure.'

Bustling away, the woman glanced back over her shoulder before turning down a side street and disappearing from view. John continued watching long after they disappeared, listening to the sounds of unrest as they came from further and further away, as he tried to calm his nerves, and wondered what he should do now.

This was not what he had signed up for. Sure, he wanted fair pay for a fair day's work, and to be treated with respect. But he could not see how causing such a disruption and damaging property would achieve those goals.

As the noise of police whistles split the air, he made up his mind. He set his feet back towards the striker's camp that had been his home for the last two weeks, ever since his shearing gang was thrown off their employer's property for refusing to work for less pay.

The camp sprawled out by the river, and was guarded by a few men who elected to stay behind to ensure they were not raided during the demonstration. In the midday heat the men gathered under a large tree, making the most of the shade. One detached himself from the group and followed John.

'You are back early, Jonno. How goes the march?'

Bill was a seasoned shearer from north of Brisbane, and had been the leading hand in John's gang. He frowned as he saw John rolling up his swag and stuffing his belongings into his pack.

'March? That is no march. It is a bunch of larrikins causing mayhem. The police came out as I left. They will all be locked up before sundown. There will be no one free to present our demands to the town council. It is a mess that will get us nowhere.'

'Ah, I did wonder… there were a few hot heads mouthing off before they even left camp. Sometimes they quieten down, other times they are egged on by the excitement of it all.'

'It was more than a few, Bill. Well, maybe it started off being just a few, but the others soon joined in. I couldn't stay. What will happen to my family if I get locked up? My mother would not be able to show her face around town, and they really need the extra money I bring in.'

'You did the right thing keeping out of trouble and coming back here, boy, but you are not planning to leave, are you? We still have a fight to win.'

'I do not see how we can win now. After today no one

around here will take us seriously. And we do not have the numbers to force a change. I can see now we are not only taking on the landholders, but our demands threaten anyone who wants to hold onto their money and position.

'Besides, I cannot afford to stay. There are only a few coins left in my pocket, and after today, the few people who offered us work will be put off.'

'John you are a bright lad with a big heart, and we need people like you to balance out those stupid enough to believe a brawl in the streets will bring about change. Stay with us and help us plan our next move.'

'I cannot, Bill. I need to think of my family and how I can make enough money to support them through the winter. Maybe it is just not our time.'

'It will never be our time if good people walk away from the fight.'

Bill's words echoed in his head as he swung his pack over his shoulder and began the long journey home.

Dappled sunlight painted the dusty ground with light and shadow. John dropped his swag and bag, and flopped under the shade of the Coolabah tree by the edge of the billabong. Placing his bag in his lap, he adjusted the bedroll into a comfortable back rest.

'Matilda, we are a sorry pair.' He laughed to himself.

When had he started calling his swag Matilda like the older shearers? Snuggling into their bedrolls of an evening, John often smiled as they traded jests about sleeping in Matilda's warm embrace.

Rummaging around in his bag, his fingers searched for the little left of his meagre supplies. Only some hard travel biscuits. *Well, at least I have enough to drink* he thought as he filled his cup from the water hole in front of him. *Hopefully I can find berries tomorrow, otherwise I will soon be going hungry.*

Chewing on one of the dry wafers and sipping his water, he leaned back against the tree trunk and shut his eyes. After the harsh reds and ochres of the Queensland outback, the blackness soothed him. Even the water had a brown hue, rather than reflecting the brilliant blue sky. Weary through and through, and not just from another day's walking, he asked himself how fate managed to bring him to this point.

Dispirited and hungry, he was heading home with only a few copper coins in his pocket. Nowhere close to the amount he expected to give his mother to tide his family over through the coming winter. His forehead creased with worry. He needed to find some work near home or they would all starve.

Before making his choice to go back to the family farm he had considered all his options. With very little to show for his time away, he worried he would become a drain on his family's meagre resources. Perhaps the quarry would hire him. After his last growth spurt he was just about as tall as a grown man, and almost as strong. That hope alone allowed him to choose returning to his family over his only other option; heading to one of the bigger towns in the hopes of picking up some labouring work.

Cursing the unions for calling the men out, now he

marvelled at how he ever believed they would improve his future. While working away, he witnessed daily how the landowners took advantage of their workers. Men who travelled far from home to shear sheep deserved better conditions and better pay than the bosses offered.

If they asked questions about falling wages, the shearers were subjected to tirades about unstable world markets, or lectures about money lost in overseas ventures. For all their grand words, employers lived in far better circumstances than those they employed. To John, it appeared in hard times unscrupulous bosses maintained their standard of living at the expense of the people who worked for them.

Sighing, he chewed thoughtfully on his biscuit. *What a mess this all is.* If only everyone would sit down and listen to each other. Yelling and fighting achieved nothing. A snap of twigs and a rustle of dry leaves interrupted his musings, and a lamb jumped out of the nearby scrub.

The animal took one look at John. 'Maaaaaaa.'

'I'm not your Ma.' John grinned at his own joke, wondering where his guest had appeared from. When he arrived earlier there had been no animals around.

'Maaaaaaa,' the young sheep insisted.

'I guess your mother must be around somewhere.'

Standing, he looked for the rest of the flock. There were no other sheep close by, and he could hear no drovers. This baby must be a stray. What should he do? Sheep stealing was illegal, yet if he left the lamb here it would surely die.

John scooped the animal up, choosing the lesser of two evils. Perhaps he would go home with something to show for his time away after all. Opening his near empty bag, he placed the lamb inside, then shoved the rest of his things around it.

He readied himself to leave, but paused as the sound of voices cut through the silence. Searching around, he found nowhere to hide. It was too late. Horses burst into the clearing and John turned to run.

'Hey, you. Halt in the name of the law.'

Hands held high, John swivelled on his heel to face the men, his back to the water. One wore military clothing, the other, from his dress, appeared to be a landholder. Both held guns aimed at him. Not knowing what to do, John began shuffling away. No shearer would be treated well by the likes of these two.

'Didn't I tell you someone had been helping themselves to my flock? And look, we caught one red handed.'

'I said stop,' the soldier commanded again. 'He will go before the magistrate, but it seems cut and dried to me. This boy will be a man before he sees freedom again.' As he smirked, John's stomach lurched.

Sheep stealing? Well, I guess I was, but I was really trying to save the lamb. They won't listen to me. Will a shearer receive an objective trial here? What about Ma? She will be mortified. How will she ever face the neighbours at church?

Broken snippets of thoughts jumbled together in his head, making it difficult to think. Backing away from the danger, soon water lapped his ankles. There was no conscious decision to continue into the water, at least not one he could remember later, but that was exactly what he did.

SWAGMAN

As if in slow motion, the trooper dismounted, stowed his rifle and grabbed a coil of rope. Tying the reigns around some scrub, he walked towards the edge of the pond. The water lazily nibbled at John's knees.

'What are you doing?' the landholder yelled, turning red, his voice rising in anger. 'Come back here.'

The water gently caressed the bottom of his bag.

'Maaaaaa,' his new pet protested, but did not struggle for release.

'Do not go any further or I'll shoot.'

He pondered how the man with the rope would shoot him without a gun, before he stumbled and his feet struggled to find purchase. Falling backwards, he splashed downwards and disappeared into the cool depths.

Arms and legs flailed as he panicked, unable to swim. As he sank deeper into the inky cold world his head spun. He marvelled, drowning appeared like being dropped from a tremendous height, and was not at all as he imagined it would be. The thought barely entered his mind before he lost it as he blacked out.

CHAPTER TWO
HEAVEN OR HELL

'Maaaa.'
There are sheep in heaven?

'Maaaa.' Something cold and wet touched his face. Water? No, it was a cold nose.

'La... La...' He forced the words out of his parched mouth as he tried to sit up. The lamb peered at him with knowing dark eyes.

Hauling himself to his feet he surveyed the clearing he had landed in. The grass gently sloped to a narrow pathway. *So this is what heaven is like?* It was green and lush compared to the harsh, dry reds and browns of Queensland. He was surrounded by green leafy trees. Although he had never seen one, he realised he was in a forest.

Through the vegetation, he made out some odd shaped buildings. *Are there towns in heaven? How come I still*

SWAGMAN

have my Matilda and bag? Will I need possessions in the great beyond? Urgently stuffing his hand into his pocket, he checked his coins were still there, just in case people used money here too.

Funny, he always thought heaven would be more white and floaty, like clouds. *Perhaps this is hell? Did I steal a lamb, and go down below instead? The preacher always told us thieves would burn in hellfire.*

Do not be so ridiculous.

'What?' John twisted around, searching for the owner of the voice. 'Who are you? Show yourself.'

'Maaaa.'

'La... La. You?' John's eyes widened as he looked more closely at the lamb.

'You call your lamb LaLa? How funny,' an amused voice intruded.

We will talk later, boy.

Again John glanced around, searching for someone to match to the new voice. Again he found no one. No one to match the mocking tones in his head, and no one to take ownership of the deeper voice in his ears. Heaven/hell was proving to be a frustrating place.

'Do you think he is dangerous?' A more feminine disembodied voice joined the conversation.

'He seems pretty harmless, and he has a name for his pet lamb. I am sure I would best him should it come to a fight,' the male voice boasted.

The undergrowth in front of him rustled, followed by some grunting, as two figures emerged through the greenery. A boy appeared first, as tall as John, but much broader. He stopped himself from laughing out loud as the lad wore a chainmail tunic and a sword belted around his hips. His clothes and swaggering stance might have leapt straight from the pages of his mother's book; *The Legends of King Arthur*.

Beside him stood a girl, hands on hips, staring down at him. He had to gulp back a laugh as she too was dressed as a character from the same stories. Wearing what appeared to be a long woollen apron over a coloured shift underneath, she was tiny, about the size of his twelve-year-old sister. However, the expression on her face and the confidence in her voice led him to believe her to be at least the same age as her companion.

Someone once told John when you drown, all the air is expelled from your body. The loss of breath must have made him light-headed, causing him to imagine things from the tales stuck in his head from days past. His mother had read to them from the well worn book of King Arthur stories every evening, and he often went to sleep dreaming he was a knight. Well, she used to, before his father died and she was too tired to do anything other than sleep after a full day's work.

'Do you think he is simple?' the girl asked her companion, not taking her eyes off him for a moment.

John heard her say the words, but her mouth formed all the wrong shapes for the sounds coming out. He shook his head, hoping the action would bring everything back to normal.

'I am not sure. Is it possible he fell out of a tree and hit his head? You can easily scramble your thoughts with a good knock. Might take a while for him to come right if that is the case.'

SWAGMAN

John's eyes widened with disbelief. The boy's mouth moved, and words were coming out, but his words also did not fit with the shape his lips were forming.

I am translating for you. Speak normally and I will make sure they understand everything you say, and vice versa.

Astonished, John watched the lamb, who stopped chewing the grass on the side of the path for a moment to stare back. He then carried on eating as though his being able to ensure people speaking different languages could understand each other was nothing out of the ordinary.

'Perhaps we should take him with us. It will be night soon, and anything might happen to him in this state.'

The boy shook his head. 'I am not sure it is a good idea given what is happening at the moment.'

'But we cannot just leave him, Stanislaus.' Her face crumpled in to a frown as she turned to John. 'Where are you from, boy? Perhaps we can take you home. We might pass it on our way back.' She directed this last comment to the young knight.

'Queensland.' Able to ignore for a moment the odd way their mouths moved when they spoke, John actually managed to answer a question.

If they are not speaking English, what are they speaking? he wondered.

French. An old version, but it is French.

'Did he say Queen's Land?' The girl turned to the boy she called Stanislaus. 'Do you know of this place?'

The boy shook his head. John noticed his hand had not left his sword since they emerged from the undergrowth.

'I have no knowledge of a queen who names her land as her own.'

'Boy, this Queen's Land, where is it? Is it far from here?' the girl asked, taking pains to make her words clear as if she spoke to a child.

'I am unable to say as I would need some idea of where here is to answer that,' John admitted. 'But I can tell you Queensland is in Australia.'

'Aus...tray...lee...a.' The girl rolled the word around in her mouth as if it was a new treat to be tried out. 'Stanislaus, you are better travelled than me. Have you been to Aus-tray-lee-a?'

The boy's gaze swung skyward as he reached for his memories. 'No, it is new to me. This is all most strange. I think Prince Henry should be told of this. It may be a foreign plot. Or at least something to do with what happened today.'

'Or it may simply be a lost boy who has banged his head and scrambled his wits.'

'I *am* lost.' More troubled now, John asked, 'Can you tell me where we are?'

'Of course we can, dunderhead. We are in the New Forest,' the girl answered.

'New Forest?' John repeated. 'Where is that?'

'The forest is large, but this section is near Romsey,' she expanded her answer.

John searched his memory. He was quite sure there was no town called Romsey in Australia. Hadn't his mother talked about a place called the New Forest? No, this could not be the same one. The woodlands she spoke of were in her home country, England.

SWAGMAN

'Are we in England?'

'Yes, we are in Briton. Where else did you think we would be, silly?' Laughing, the girl placed her hand on her companion's arm. 'Stanislaus, I think he needs to come with us. His wits are addled. He cannot be left alone. If he died because we did nothing, well I do not want his death on my conscience.'

Still confused, John could not believe people in England dressed this differently to people in Australia. Then a thought occurred to him.

'What is the date?'

Stanislaus stood in silence for a moment before answering, 'The second day of August in the year of Our Lord, 1100.' The boy followed this with a decisive nod of his head. 'I believe you are right. If he does not even know the date, he must be very confused. He needs to see a healer at least. We can take him with us and ask Master Gavin to examine him when we get back?'

Without even asking for his input, the strangely dressed boy picked up John's swag and his bedroll from where they had fallen on the ground, and took him firmly by the arm, raising him to his feet. 'Come on, our wagon is this way. We must hurry, we are already late and our news is really important.'

'Oh, Stanislaus, quit complaining. It is hardly my fault the Mother Superior needed wood chopped. You should be pleased you could help.'

'You could have spoken out for me though. You could have told her we did not have time because we needed to get back and report to the prince.'

The boy's petulant tones barely penetrated John's

thoughts as he pondered how he ended up in England, in the Middle Ages. For all he knew heaven/hell might replicate something from your imagination so you did not feel scared when you arrived. Well, it wasn't working.

As they walked along the path, John glanced over his shoulder to find his fluffy companion following along. With the boy and girl in front continuing their banter, he took the opportunity to test something.

Have you any idea where we are going? He formed the words inside his head, imagining speaking them slowly and clearly so he could be easily understood.

Of course I do, the voice in his mind projected disdain. *But you have not asked the right question.*

John shook his head, bemused not only by the oddity of talking to a lamb, but that the animal was instructing him. The right question? Was he to believe there was a right question in this situation?

Am I dead?

What do you think?

I fell into a billabong and I did not rise to the surface. It is not out of the question to believe I am dead.

I am disappointed. I searched long and hard for you. Well, a version of you I could use given the circumstances we are in. Unfortunately on first meeting I find you are not as intelligent and open minded as I anticipated. The lamb paused and looked up at him, as though assessing his worth.

SWAGMAN

He was not going to take being judged by a sheep of unknown origins without a fight. *I am disappointed for you, truly I am. Perhaps thinking of this from my point of view might give you some perspective. If I am not dead, then the only other option is I fell through water into Medieval England with a talking lamb, to be aided by a knight and a lady. Death or fantasy, which is more likely?*

I understand that where you come from, with your limited experience of the universe and all its permutations, your answer would be death. However, if you would open your mind a little and consider things from my point of view, the answer would be completely different. With these words the lamb obviously considered the subject closed as he continued on after the others.

Annoyed with what he considered to be an insult, but unable to think of a suitable response, John wandered along behind. When the group emerged from the forest path, he put his resentment aside as he dealt with the new situation.

Stanislaus dropped John's gear into the back of a rustic farm cart parked beside the dirt track, and walked over to a draft horse picketed nearby, calmly eating grass. As the knight tethered the horse to the cart, the lamb roughly head-butted John's leg.

I am happy to travel in your bag.

Without thinking, John picked up the lamb and settled him inside.

'You can ride in the back,' the girl instructed as she climbed up to sit on the front seat beside Stanislaus. Once John had settled himself safely on board, the lamb snuggled in the pack beside him, the cart lurched forward and they were on their way.

As they travelled, John's thoughts once again focused on attempting to figure out what had happened to him. Which, unfortunately, meant once again talking to the lamb.

So, I am not dead? John asked.

No, you are most certainly not.

I am in Medieval England?

Yes.

How?

That is the wrong question.

John almost groaned out loud in frustration. *No, it is not. The answer is important to me.*

It does not help your situation knowing you fell through a time and place portal I created. You need to ask a different question.

Or you could just tell me what I need to learn.

Or you might think of this as a test. I want to observe how your mind works to be reassured you are up to doing this. Again the voice in his head sounded more like a teacher than a farm animal.

In his annoyance John briefly considered not asking the obvious question. His silence did not last long as he truly did want to find out what he was doing here. What was the right question to get the answer he needed? He fell through a thing called a portal to Medieval England. Ah...

Why? Why am I here, and what do you want me to do? Is that the right question? John grinned, sure now he was right.

Finally we are getting somewhere. I brought you here for a specific purpose. I cannot tell you exactly what it is

SWAGMAN

because events must unfold of their own accord. For the moment though, while we assess the lay of the land, I need you to stop acting like a simpleton and start acting normal.

Frowning, John responded, *Yes, because it is so normal walking around in clothes from 600 years in the future with a sheep in tow.*

Nearly 800 years, the lamb snorted. *And you may laugh about my form, but in this time, it is quite common for people to bring farm animals with them when they travel. They are way more valuable now than in your time. Besides, as a lamb people will take little notice of me, and I can better observe what is going on.*

John's stomach lurched as he remembered how he came to be in possession of the lamb. *Will people think I stole you? I mean, I did actually take you when we were in future Australia.*

His companion cocked his head to the side as he thought this over. *Actually, you did not take me, I took you. However, I guess we cannot totally rule out someone thinking I am stolen. Though you are well enough dressed for this period, so no doubt people will assume you can afford to own a valuable animal.*

Oh... umm. All right. If you are sure then. John was not fully convinced, but the lamb's voice was authoritative, and his travelling companions already assumed the animal was with him and raised no questions, so he decided he had far more pressing things to worry about.

If we are to be in whatever we are in together, I guess I should ask your name. Do you have a name?

Lala is as good a name as any.

Really? You do not think it makes me sound like a

simpleton.

'Boy. BOY. Are you still all right? Stanislaus, he looks a little strange. Stop the cart, we should check on him.'

'No, I am fine.' Jolted from his internal conversation by the increasing volume of her voice, John answered then fell over as Stanislaus turned to check on him and the cart swerved onto rough ground.

'Stanislaus, watch where you are going. If you put another cart in a ditch you will not be allowed out without a driver again.'

From his place in the back, it sounded as though the girl was laughing, rather than being as distressed as her words made her out to be.

'It was not my fault, it was Alain's,' Stanislaus grumbled as he concentrated on his driving. 'He said turn left here, how was I to guess he meant at the crossroad ahead, not where we were? Surely I cannot be blamed for his poor directions.'

A snort erupted from John's mouth before he could stop it, and it soon turned into full blown laughter as he imagined the incident his driver described.

'At least you have a sense of humour, boy.' His reaction had gained the lady's approval.

'John. You can call me John,' he offered, tired of being called *boy* like some servant.

'And you may call me Barabal. This big oaf is Stanislaus. Are you feeling better?'

Good, this is more normal. Do not muck this up, we need their help.

Shh, I am talking with actual people here.

'I am, thank you. The knock to my head appeared to

be worse than I first thought.' Using the idea they had given him, he explained away his earlier behaviour.

'Do you remember where you are from yet?'

'It is funny, but I cannot.' Fortunately John remembered in medieval times Australia had not yet been discovered, but he did not know enough about the period to think up an alternative. In the meantime, losing his memory appeared to be the best option until he found somewhere far enough away to call home and not be caught out in a lie. As a bonus, if they thought he had amnesia there was a chance they would not ask too many questions.

'You can only remember your name?'

'Yes.'

'Not where you were going?'

'No,' John replied, wondering why Barabal was asking so many questions.

'Did you see anything odd on your travels?'

'Barabal, he cannot remember the day or how he fell, how would he remember that. Prince Henry will want to speak with him regardless of what he saw or did not see,' Stanislaus explained. 'Even if all this was not a little odd considering what has happened, he is bound to want to talk to any stranger who showed up in the area, today of all days.'

'We will take him to Master Gavin first though, will we not?' Although presented as a question, the tone implied it was more of an order. The other boy showed he understood it in the same way.

'Yes, ma'am.' The smirk in the knight's voice caused a smile. 'Anyway, Alain said he had something to show me, something about making a bang and breaking things.

It sounds exciting.'

'I am not sure you two should be left alone together.' Barabal shook her head.

John's ears pricked at the mention of Alain, he was interested in meeting someone who knew how to blow things up.

And Alain makes four.

What do you mean?

Soon, my young helper, soon.

John dozed a little, the rocking of the wagon encouraging sleep. Having walked for most of the day, his body was tired when he stopped to rest under the Coolabah tree. Then being flung around in the water hole and thrown back in time to a country on the other side of the world had exhausted his last store of energy. His body craved a good night's rest.

The wagon came to an abrupt stop, jolting him awake. He forced his eyes open and found himself on the drawbridge of a real, live castle.

CHAPTER THREE
CASTLES AND WIZARDS ARE REAL!

Stanislaus steered the cart through the opening and into the castle's bailey, deftly moving around the people and animals milling in the courtyard. Everywhere John looked men and women rushed around. However, in spite of the frantic activity, the mood was sombre. Maybe in medieval England, people went round with long faces all the time, but this did not feel normal.

'See, I told you we would not be far behind the party accompanying the coal burner's cart.' Barabal turned triumphantly to Stanislaus.

'They obviously travelled more slowly to allow villagers to pay their respects.'

'Did someone die?'

As he considered the possibility a death would explain why people were so sad John fell, almost hitting his head on the seat in front as the cart lurched when his companions turned and stared in amazement.

'How can you not know?'

'Barabal, how would I have any idea who died? Many people die every day.'

'The king was shot with an arrow while hunting,' Stanislaus explained as he was called around the back of the castle towards what turned out to be a stable. In the cobbled space in front of a barn door, a boy took hold of the horse and waited for them to get down from the cart.

Is that why I am here? The king's death?

Partially, yes, but more because of the way he died. Pay attention and you will learn more.

'Master Black is not happy,' the boy holding onto the horse informed Stanislaus. 'He demanded an explanation when you returned. You were gone way longer than you said, and after last time...'

'He can take it up with Prince Henry,' Stanislaus retorted sharply, looking down his nose at the lad. 'After what happened to King William he sent us on an errand, and that took as long as it took.'

Without a backwards glance, the knight stalked away, with no offer of help and without further thought for the boy left behind to tend to his horse. His arrogance reminded John of the landowners in Australia, and he squirmed with discomfort as he followed behind the knight.

It is the way of nobility everywhere. Things can change if nudged in the right direction at the right time.

Looking down at the lamb he was carrying he thought, *Is that what I am doing here? Nudging things in the right direction?*

SWAGMAN

Only time will tell. The baby sheep settled more comfortably in the bag, closed his eyes and drifted off to sleep, if the sound of gentle snores were anything to go by.

The castle was a maze of wood and stone outbuildings, set around a central grand hall called the castle keep. Following Stanislaus and Barabal through the throng of people towards one of the larger dwellings attached to the keep, he shivered in the chilly evening air.

It had been warm in Queensland, and the day still had some heat when he arrived in this strange place. Now, with the sun's disappearance, the temperature had dropped considerably to a bone chilling level he had not experienced before. This weather was colder than a Queensland winter. Which was odd, as the leaves were still green, and the sun's heat during the day suggested autumn had not yet reached England.

As he walked through the corridor, John's nose creased in distaste as a horrendous odour hit him; a combination of damp wool, rotten vegetables and cooked meat. He had thought sharing a dormitory with shearers who seldom bathed was bad enough, but the stench assaulting his nose was overwhelming. He was forced to concentrate on keeping the contents of his stomach inside, where they belonged.

Finally they came to a small wooden door, opening into a room lined floor to ceiling with jars and bottles. The unpleasant aroma abated as he was hit with the sweetness of fresh herbs. Searching for the source of his relief, John glanced up and saw bundles of plants drying in bunches hung from the roof. Stanislaus closed the door behind them, only for it to be flung open seconds later, nearly knocking them all over. A small man burst through the opening and dropped the basket he was carrying on the table before he realised anyone else was there.

'A... ah... Stanislaus, Barabal... and, umm... do I know you?' The man squinted at John as if trying to place where he had seen him before.

'Master Gavin, this is John. We found him on the road. He had a bit of a fall and cannot remember where he is from.' Barabal pushed him from behind. 'We thought you might check him over and do something to bring his memories back.'

Master Gavin frowned, peering closely at John. 'I can take a look Barabal, but it is generally only time that returns memories after a knock to the head.

'Perhaps someone local knows him and could help, although I can tell from the manner of his clothing he is not from around here. Maybe he is from across the sea? Squire Stanislaus, have you seen clothing like this before?'

Everyone appeared to treat the squire as the font of knowledge on things foreign. He shook his head.

'He is not from Normandie and he does not dress like anyone I have ever seen in my master's court, or anywhere else I have travelled.'

Gavin frowned more deeply, a furrow etching itself between his brows. 'You two had best be getting back to our future king. He has been asking where you are, and you know he does not like to be kept waiting. When you have reported, come back and I should be able to tell you more about your friend.'

Stanislaus headed for the door, but Barabal lingered a minute longer. 'You will be fine here. Master Gavin is the best apothecary for miles.' She gave a brief smile as she left for her important meeting with the future king.

'Put your bag down young man and let us take a look at you.'

The apothecary had a surprisingly firm grip as he took John's arm and led him over to a stool by the fire, where he placed the other hand on his shoulder, encouraging him to sit on a none-too-stable seat.

John dropped his bag on the rush covered ground beside him. Lala nuzzled his way out through the opening and stretched his legs, then ambled over to the fire, curling up in the warmth preparing to sleep. In reality, his black eyes watched Master Gavin with intelligent interest.

The master's examination consisted of touching all around his head, paying particular attention to the sides. He frowned and grunted as he went, but said nothing at all to John.

'Mmm,' the shorter man said under his breath. 'No lump. Unusual for a case of memory loss.'

He walked around John, and the boy turned to watch what he was doing, causing the stool to wobble. Medieval furniture was not suitable for someone of his build.

'Not made for one as big as you, eh? Now let us find the bump. Does it hurt anywhere in particular?'

John shook his head as the man's fingers began their search again, this time pressing a little harder. 'I cannot feel anything out of the ordinary.' The fingers on his head stopped moving and something warm trickled into his skull.

Throwing the hands off as he leapt to his feet, John gasped, 'What the...?'

Nothing to be worried about he was only checking inside your head.

But... but...

'Sorry, I forgot. I should have warned you it was time for an internal exam.' Master Gavin frowned again. 'Sit. Sit. I am almost done.'

John sat. A large rush of warmth encased him, and he realised he was unable to move, not even to wiggle a finger.

'What... what are you...' At least his mouth was still operational, even if his brain could not process what the man had done.

Gavin moved around to face him, hands on hips. 'I find nothing wrong with your head, and I suspect your memory loss is a ruse. I need the truth. These are troubled times, and we cannot tolerate spies in our midst.'

John stared warily at the man, whose eyes were now only slightly above his own.

'What have you done to me?' Shrugging and wriggling, he attempted to loosen the bonds holding him in place.

'Nothing harmful, just something to protect me while I find out the truth of you. Who are you and what are you doing here?'

'I will tell you what I told the others. I am John Smith, and I am from Queensland. They did not believe me, and I do not expect you to either. They thought I was insane, but they stopped fussing when I told them I lost my memory.'

Master Gavin stood still, the flickering of his eyes the only sign he was mulling over John's answer. 'Mmm, odd. Very odd indeed. I sense you are telling the truth, but this Queen's Land of yours is not a place I recollect. How did you get here? By ship?'

SWAGMAN

John paused before answering, wondering what to say. The truth would make him sound even more crazy, but the apothecary seemed to be able to tell whether or not he lied. Sighing, he decided to take a plunge and go with the truth.

'I am told I fell through a time and place portal. Apparently I am here to help events unfold in the right direction.'

John expected Gavin to laugh at the very least, or name him a madman at worst, but the man merely continued to stare at him, his eyes doing the strange flickering thing again. Finally the man's stance relaxed and the bonds around John loosen, but did not fall away entirely.

'I asked The Guardians for help to make sure this change goes well for the people of Briton. They suffered so under King William the Second, and deserve better this time around. Are you who they sent? How can you help us? You are but a boy.'

'I have no idea whether or not I can help you,' John admitted. 'I come from some time in your future where I jumped into a billabong—a pond—and I ended up here. Although I understand I am near the New Forest in medieval times, I am not sure I completely understand where *here* is. I can tell you though, if you need help and I can aid you, I will do what I am able to.'

'In what year did you jump into the pond with the funny name?'

Once again John did not know what to say. This whole story sounded absurd even to his own ears, he could only imagine what Master Gavin was thinking. If he told him the truth, the man would surely think him mad.

'Come, come boy. I am one of the few who is aware there are special people who can travel through time, so you can tell me. Although I must warn you to be careful not to reveal this to anyone else as they will think you addle-brained.

'You already said you come from the future, I am only asking how far into that future you have travelled back from.'

Still a little reluctant to answer, John realised as a captive he needed to say something. He opted for the truth again, and mumbled, '1890.'

'Good Lord! You came from that far forward? There are so many questions I need to ask you. So much you can teach me.'

It was the first time John had seen the man's face do anything but frown. His eyes glittered with excitement and his hands shook as he contemplated the possibilities a boy from the future offered.

No, you must understand knowledge of future events and inventions is not allowed.

John started. He had all but forgotten Lala was in the room. To his surprise, Master Gavin also appeared thrown by the interruption. Still only able to move his head, John looked at the lamb and raised an eyebrow.

Those with gifts can also hear me. Did I not tell you? Clearly you did not.

'Who is talking in my head? It sounds like you, but your lips are not moving' he pointed at John. 'Someone else is here too.' He glanced around, his eyes coming to rest on the animal by the fire. 'Great One?' he asked in wonder.

SWAGMAN

You can call me Lala, as the boy does.

'Great One?' John asked.

'You do not comprehend the honour bestowed on you? You are travelling with one of the protectors of the earth. One of the Time Guardians.' Gavin was astonished.

'I do not know what one of those is,' John replied tartly, wondering what all the fuss was about.

In his time, they no longer remember the protectors of the earth. Although we are no longer revered we are still around, carrying out our work protecting the timeline. It will not surprise you to find they also lost the use of their gifts. If this one were born now, he would be an adept, perhaps stronger. As it is, he is the best I could bring to help you on such short notice. King William the Second was not meant to die this soon, and we were unprepared for the event when you called for assistance.

A long silence followed Lala's speech. Master Gavin shook his head, sadness and disbelief vying for rights to his face. Turning back to John, he waved his hand and the bonds fell away.

'I do not want to be told anything about your time. You do not revere the timeless ones who protect the world, and you squander the gift. Your time has no respect for the things I hold dear.'

Able to move now, John felt reluctant to stand. 'So you mean to tell me, not only did I fall through a time and place portal, but the lamb I fell with is some sort of special being? And I am also to believe you are what? A wizard?'

'I prefer Druid, if you do not mind.'

'I am beginning to wish I had actually drowned,' John said as his head sunk into his hands.

If a lamb could be said to laugh, Lala was definitely doing just that. His mouth was open and he was emitting a strange sort of bleating, choking noise. Eventually he gained control of himself and was back to business.

Come now. There is little time and much for us to do. It is important we bring Master Gavin up to date on what is happening.

'Master Gavin? What about me? Surely I need to learn more about what is going on.'

That is simple. Today William Rufus, the second king of Briton by that name, was killed while out hunting. Those with him when he passed are being spare with the details of the event, consequently no one is saying whether or not it was an accident or regicide.

In fact, at the moment, no one is one hundred percent sure who sent the fatal arrow, and there are many potential candidates. He was not a good king and he had many enemies. His brother, Prince Henry, third son of William the Conqueror, is set to take over the throne, in spite of his older brother, Duke Robert Curthose of Normandie, having the stronger claim.

'And you want me to stop Prince Henry from stealing the crown?' John interrupted.

Master Gavin's head jerked up in shock. 'Good Lord, no. Tell me you did not bring him here to stop Prince Henry from taking the throne? That is not why I called for help. I want to make sure Prince Henry is crowned, anything else would be a disaster.

'The people want someone who is going to reduce taxation and strengthen the laws of the kingdom so the barons are kept in check. Henry is the only man who can achieve those aims. Many of the dukes and barons support that fat, lazy Robert Curthose. He would think nothing of bleeding us dry to fund his crusades and border disputes, while the barons run riot.'

'So if he is who the people want to rule them, why do you need me?' John asked.

Why? Because the people will have very little say in the transfer of power. Many of the barons want Robert Curthose to be king because he would not be able to control them, allowing them to do as they wished. Members of the Clergy would also see the disarray as an opportunity to snatch back power lost under King William the Second. The people fear this more than anything.

Then there are those who would prefer the return of an Anglo-Saxon King. Although there are no strong contenders, they would do anything to have one of their own back on the throne. A power struggle would also not benefit the people.

The future of Briton sits on a knife edge, and we are here to ensure a smooth transition for Prince Henry.

'If no one wants him to be king, why are we supporting him?'

In the original timeline, Prince Henry was acknowledged as King William the Second's heir before he died, and took the crown unopposed on the king's death. He is a learned man, and spent much of his rule establishing a new justice for landholders. Unbeknownst to him, he began the process of devolving power from the crown and the ruling classes to the people.

'If I am hearing you correctly, all the powers in the land want Duke Robert Curthose as king? I am but one boy. What can I do in the face of such opposition?'

Henry is moving fast to win over those who are against his taking the throne. He is talking to the Church, promising to give up the practice of appointing clergy to vacant post and returning this right to the bishops. This small concession of power, and income, will bring many over to his side. Lala paused to drink from a bowl Master Gavin placed in front of him, before continuing.

Some of the barons support him—those who do not want to see Briton fall into disarray, or be subjugated by a Norman prince more interested in the Crusades than his own lands on the continent. They fear Briton will be stripped of its resources to support his other interests. Those barons are working to win more of their colleagues over to their side, but Prince Henry will need to do more before he can be certain of their support. However, there is little we can do to help him in that area. We must rely on him being able to give them a little more independence, and perhaps forgive their debts to the crown, to achieve his goals.

The final prong to his campaign is where we come in. Henry aims to marry the King of Scotland's sister, as her Anglo-Saxon blood will swing many towards his side. Stanislaus and Barabal were assisting with this today. They went to visit the princess in Romsey Abbey. However, she will not wed unless he introduces a system of local courts they discussed when they first met, and he is not sure he wants to go this far with reform so soon.

We need to ensure Matilda and Henry pledge to marry, thus uniting enough of the ruling classes behind them for him to take the crown. This is the only way to ensure the first step in dispersing some of the royal power. Without Prince Henry on the throne, there will be no Magna Carta, no votes for all men and no votes for women. Lala stopped, placed his head on the side, and looked at Gavin and John.

'Firstly, we here in Briton know Princess Matilda by the name she prefers: Edith. If you call her Matilda, very few will know who you are talking about.

'Secondly, I only wanted to see Prince Henry crowned. I did not realise he was going to be so important for the future. Because of him, common men will get a say in government at some stage.' Master Gavin was wide-eyed with amazement. 'Votes for women though? Are you sure? In all honesty I do not think women choosing leaders would be a good idea. Their brains are not designed for making such important decisions as choosing rulers.'

'Tell that to my mother.' John laughed. 'She says she runs a farm just like a man and yet has no say in choosing the government, or in how the taxes she pays are spent.'

Turning to the lamb he asked, 'Lala, how am I supposed to help with this? I could not do anything about the problems in Queensland caused by the strike.

'I ran away because, although I agreed with their aims, I was worried about the violence and how it would all end up. When I tried to talk to others about peaceful solutions, they did not want to listen to the lone voice of a mere boy.'

It is because you recognised violence was not the

solution that you are perfect for this. There is a cost to change, there always is, but in the end peaceful change is more lasting.

'All right, suppose I am the right person, what can one boy do?'

Not one boy, but four people. Barabal and Stanislaus have been in contact with the future queen and are already working to bring Prince Henry together with his bride. You will join them and Alain to make sure Prince Henry is betrothed to Princess Matilda—umm Edith—then crowned.

'Do you not think it funny the future Queen of Briton has the same name as a swag?' Hysterical laughter bubbled up inside, bursting out before John could stop it. Amazed they could not see the joke, he attempted to appear more serious when he found Master Gavin and Lala observing him as though the strain had become too much, and he had lost his mind.

Swallowing his laughter, he said, 'Perhaps we should stick to calling her Princess Edith? If only because I cannot say her name without falling into fits of giggles.' When there was no response he asked, 'Have you any idea exactly what I need to do?'

No, Lala admitted. *Given the mix up with time, all I can be certain of is you need to be here to intervene in some way. I can only assume your role will become clearer the more we learn. Initially you can support Barabal, Stanislaus and Alain.*

'Alain? My apprentice? Are you sure? He is more often than not a little vague. Spends most of his time tinkering and inventing things. Not the type you would rely on to save the day.'

SWAGMAN

His unique way of looking at a problem will be essential if we are to achieve the right outcome for the people.

'I still do not understand why you brought me here from another time. There must be plenty of people around who can help the others.' Working through all the details in his head, John could not see why someone from the future was needed to resolve this problem.

You come from a time and place where the changes we want to occur are taken for granted. In fact, some might go as far as to say the basic tenets of fairness have begun to be eroded by landholders, and that you and your shearing friends are fighting for fairness to be restored. Your passion and insight about what might be lost here may just be what is needed to tip the scales, and bring about the changes we need.

Now enough chatting, I think it is time you met the future King of Briton.

Lala stood on gangly legs and wobbled across the room, followed by Master Gavin and John.

'Will people not think it strange a lamb wandering the halls?' John asked Master Gavin.

'Would an animal in a dwelling be thought strange in your time?' The master raised his eyebrows.

'Umm, yes,' John answered. 'Especially in a palace.'

'Well, I never. Where do you keep your live stock in bad weather?'

'In the barn if we have a really bad storm, but sheep roam outside all year for the most part.'

Astonished, Master Gavin stopped still. 'You leave something as valuable as a sheep outside in the elements all year? How wealthy your land must be if you do not

worry about your stock going missing.'

'I guess it is not so odd for a lamb to be here with me after all.' Once again reminded of the strangeness of this place, John followed Lala into the main hall where Prince Henry, the future king, was holding court.

CHAPTER FOUR
MEETING THE FUTURE KING

Gavin and John eased themselves in behind a group of men milling around in the packed great hall of the palace, ensuring there was enough space between them to protect Lala from stray feet. Nearly stumbling through the rushes strewn on the floor, Gavin righted John before he could fall into one of the richly dressed nobles. Wrinkling his nose as he regained his footing, he wished he had a handkerchief to press to his face like many of the noblemen were.

'Don't they believe in bathing?' he muttered under his breath.

Gavin leaned in. 'Of course they do, it is just when so many people are gathered together in one place it is difficult for servants to be able to accommodate regular baths for everyone, what with heating cauldrons over the fire, then carrying them to the bathing room. A court visit increases their workload, in fact they did not get around to changing the rushes on the floor in here today, I could smell the stench when I entered the building. No doubt they will not get an opportunity until the nobles are well in their beds.

'We are a sleepy little castle between royal visits. When the nobles roll into town the servants work dawn til dusk and beyond to ensure everyone's comfort as best as they are able.'

Suitably chastised, John attempted to hide his embarrassment by surveying the room. He had not considered how people would bath without a tub and running water, nor how they would clean a castle filled to the brim with guests.

The druid had found them a position along a wall to the side of the room near the back. They had a little space and could see over the heads of the assembled nobles of the land to a platform at the other end. Winchester's great hall was a large, rectangular room with a balcony level running around the two long sides and across the back. Opposite them were other people in poorer dress, perhaps senior castle workers like Master Gavin, or lesser nobles. With faces turned towards the man standing in prayer on the dais directly in front of the door, they all waited.

As the man communed with God, John studied him. Shorter than most, he was slight of form but when he stood, he moved as someone confident in their physical ability. Although no one would call Prince Henry good looking, there was something about the dark haired man that drew you to him. Maybe it was the intensity and intelligence of his startling blue eyes. Flanking him were two men dressed only a little less flamboyantly than the prince himself.

'Robert de Beaumont, a supporter of the Prince's, and Ranulf Flambard, the late king's close advisor,' Gavin whispered when he saw the direction of John's gaze.

'There are an awful lot of noble looking people here,' he commented.

'Most of Briton's high and mighty came when King William Rufus called the barons to court. The hunt today was by way of a welcome. A feast had been planned for tonight... all that food gone to waste...'

'How very convenient for him to die with so many barons here to ratify a new king.' The words came out louder than he expected, and he was rewarded with a glare from the man standing in front of them.

'Your thoughts are not something I would voice out loud while suspicious rumours circulate about King William's death,' Gavin admonished.

'You don't mean...' John turned to look at the druid. 'You do not think that Prince Henry killed his brother?'

Lala answered, *Henry may be named Beauclerc because of his scholarly leanings, but make no mistake, the man can wield a sword and bow along with the best of them.*

John thought about his own family and could not imagine being able to kill any of them, no matter how annoying they were. 'I cannot believe anyone would kill their own family members,' he finally said.

Master Gavin drew himself up tall, and spoke in the same tone many of John's teachers had used when lecturing in class. *Brothers they may have been, but no love was lost between William the Conqueror's three sons. Why, King William the Second and Duke Robert Curthose joined together to throw Prince Henry off the lands in Normandie he had legally purchased from his brother with his inheritance. This detente between Henry and King William was a recent thing.*

John interrupted, *Still, to kill your own brother, you risk burning in hell for all eternity.*

Lala answered, *True, and to be fair, Prince Henry is not the only man here holding a grudge against the king. Almost everyone in this room had a reason to want the man gone, especially as many believe this court was called for King William to raise another tax on the gentry. Now hush, I want to listen to the prince.* The lamb ended their conversation.

John turned his attention back to the stage, finding Prince Henry was waiting for quiet so he could speak.

'Dark days are on us when a king is felled by a stray arrow while hunting. I know many of you are calling this a judgement from God for the ungodly actions of my brother. Many of you are also alleging his death was not accidental, looking amongst our number for someone to cast blame upon. We detained the man who shot the fateful arrow. If we are to keep our country from falling into disarray, all speculation about events today must stop until we have had time to question him.

'Upon finding my brother's dead body, I realised we needed to move quickly. My first priority was to ensure the country stayed strong, and to prevent our neighbours taking advantage of the situation. I rushed back here to attend to matters of state. Then spent the afternoon ensuring our Welsh border was fully manned, and I want to thank those of you who escorted the king's body back for your thoughtfulness. It warms my heart to know he did not take that final journey alone.'

'Rushed back to secure the royal treasury more like,' the man in front of John whispered to his neighbour, who chuckled his appreciation.

'We have much to do over the next few months,' Henry Beauclerc continued over muttered comments from the floor. 'However, we are now in mourning for our departed king, and I would ask you to leave off your politicking until we bury my brother.' He half-turned and gestured to the body laid out on the long table behind.

'You will not have to wait long. Tomorrow will see him buried in the cathedral here at Winchester, as befits a king of our land.'

'Will we not wait for Archbishop Anselm to arrive to perform the service?' someone in front of Henry asked so all could hear.

William de Breteuil, one of Robert Curthose's men. John looked down to see Lala standing by his feet. *We need to be wary of him.*

'As you are all aware, we are in early spring so our days are warm, and my brother took an arrow to the gut. His body deteriorates as we speak. For our king's dignity, we cannot wait days until the archbishop arrives.

'Now, we are all weary and I would like some time to mourn my brother alone.'

A clear note of dismissal rang through his voice. Amidst grumblings and arguments, the assembled lords left the hall and headed to their accommodation in

Winchester. A man in rich clerical robes remained near the front as the others departed. Handing him a small pouch heavy with coins, the prince invited him onto the platform to pray for his brother's soul.

Master Gavin nudged John towards the platform where Barabal and Stanislaus stood waiting for Prince Henry to take note of their presence. Barabal smiled briefly at John as he came up behind them, but was then called to speak with the future king by the man Master Gavin had called Robert de Beaumont. Stanislaus' shoulders dropped as he remained behind with them.

'No one ever thinks I have anything to offer,' the young squire grumbled.

'Shh,' Master Gavin hushed him. 'I cannot make out what they are saying.'

Stanislaus glared daggers at the druid, but Master Gavin ignored him, turning his attention to the man he hoped would become the king of Briton.

'Ah, Mistress Barabal, did you find Princess Edith in good spirits?'

'She was well, sire, and not too saddened to learn of the death of your brother the king.' Barabal dropped into a curtsey as she spoke.

Henry Beauclerc laughed in appreciation. 'Please rise, Barabal, we are informal here. I will not trouble you to relay her message word for word, that lady made clear her opinion of my brother to all who would listen. So what about the matter I sent you to discuss with her?' A single eyebrow rose in query.

'Well... sire...' For someone who had previously had so much to say, Barabal now appeared lost for words, peeking John's interest. Was this a potential problem?

'You may speak plainly with me, Barabal, I will not punish the messenger if the message is displeasing.'

Barabal took a deep breath. 'Sire, the lady will consider your offer, after she receives the full details of your proposal.'

'What more is there to say?' Prince Henry was genuinely puzzled. 'I offer the lady the crown of Briton as my wife. How could I possibly make my intentions more clear?'

'Forgive me, sire, there is more to her message. The lady requires you confirm the vision you share and your plan on how to bring it to fruition, in writing, before she will say yes.'

'Goddam the woman,' Prince Henry spluttered. 'How often have we spoken of our shared dream for Briton? Is it not obvious I chose her for my bride because she has been vocal in support of my ideals? Why must I put it down in writing to be believed?'

'If I may be so bold, sire?' Barabal interjected. 'Her exact words were, "If I am to leave a life of contemplation and learning and take up the mantle of Queen of Briton, I need reassurances I will have a true role in government and Henry has a clear vision of the first steps he will take to allow more localised self-government. I am sure he will be angry when you tell him this, but I am a mere woman in a man's world and I want contractual assurances".' Barabal shuffled uncomfortably after delivering Princess

Edith's words, waiting for the prince's explosive reaction.

Laughter rang through the room. Deep, throaty, joyous laughter. 'And that is why Edith is the wife I need at my side as I take the crown of Briton. Not only will she bring me support from Anglo-Saxon dissenters, she will also back my changes allowing landholders a level of self-governance, which will bring better justice for all men. Best of all though, she is pragmatic and plain spoken. I really could not spend the rest of my life with a simpering fool, forever guessing what they want from me.'

Robert de Beaumont did not appear to be as happy about the situation as his friend. 'Henry, today you sent a letter to Archbishop Anselm offering a return of the allocation of clerical vacancies to the church in return for their support.

'I know the barons are straining under heavy taxation and you assured them you would wind down activity on the Welsh border. You even hinted at forgiving their existing debts to the crown. Then you let the barons know you were not against giving them back control of arranging marriages.

'Any one of these actions reduces the amount in your coffers, both now and in the future, while boosting the power of the barons and the church. You will gain many supporters as a result of those actions, so the cost is well worth it.

'If they then find you want to reduce their authority and income by allowing landowners to hold their own courts in the hundreds, you may lose some of them again. Is that wise?'

John watched Prince Henry as he stood, unmoving,

stroking his beard.

Lala, I know of barons, but what are the hundreds?

They are smaller divisions of the land a baron controls, usually used for organising military contributions to the crown. King Edmund the First allowed local courts in the hundreds with a system allowing local landholders to administer their own justice. Prince Henry always talks about restoring that institution, and Princess Edith supported his view whenever they chanced to meet. The Scots have always been more progressive than the English when it comes to sharing power.

'Well, perhaps we do not need to tell them of that particular plan quite yet. We can wait until I have the crown placed on my head.'

'Umm... excuse me, sire, I have more.' Was Barabal blushing? 'The lady also said to tell you in return for your full restoration of Edmund the Confessor's legal system, she would bear your children, and agree to turn a blind eye to your other... umm... dalliances.' Barabal's face was now scarlet, and she would not meet the Prince's eyes.

What?

Our Prince Henry is a man who, let us say, enjoys the company of women. So much so he has not married for fear it would restrict his activities. Oh, he says he is still a bachelor because he is a pauper with nothing to offer a bride, but in reality, no good woman would put up with his affairs.

Oh. John felt the heat rising up his neck towards his face, and he sympathised with Barabal having to raise such a delicate topic.

Again Henry laughed. 'Edith knows me well. Robert,

I must give much to gain the support of the barons lest too many of them decide my oldest brother is a better option for the crown, simply because they can run roughshod over him.

'This marriage though, this I do for myself and the Princess Edith. We both are better off not tied to anyone, but if we need to be married it should be to people who allow us to be ourselves. If the price of that is instituting courts in the hundreds, then so be it.

'Although, I do strongly believe landholders deserve the right to settle affairs in their local areas. Many of my brother's barons are getting fat off their lands, while their people suffer the consequences. Ruling as they see fit, without recourse to the laws of Briton, their excesses must be curbed. Once I have given them a little something at the top to sweeten them up, I will then take from the bottom to restrict their power and show my strength. It will keep them on their toes.'

Without thinking through his actions, John found himself stepping forward and interrupting, 'What about the men who own no land? Are they to be given any concessions?'

What are you doing? Lala asked as all eyes in the room turned to John. Master Gavin stepped away from his side, physically distancing himself from the boy's ill considered words.

CHAPTER FIVE
CASTLES REALLY DO HAVE DUNGEONS

In the silence, Henry's eyes bored deep into John's, the power in them almost forcing the boy to step back.

'Who are you to talk to your betters without invitation?' the prince asked as he advanced towards the edge of the dais.

'Begging your pardon, Prince Henry.' Stanislaus stepped in front of John, shielding him from the intense scrutiny for a moment. 'We found this boy on the road after he bumped his head, and he is still not in his right mind. He only spoke out of turn because he is addled-brained.'

Henry frowned, and started to turn away, but John continued.

'If you give this power to the landholders, they will use it to abuse the common man. And in the long run you will cause more trouble for those the barons abuse now.'

John, hold your tongue. You are fighting for something more than we need at this point in history. Lala's voice rang in his head, halting his outburst for a moment while he answered the lamb.

Lala, it is because the landholders are given such powers they think they can walk all over the shearers. Perhaps if all men are included in the court system now, we can avoid the shearer's strike in my time.

John had never experienced a silence like this, it was if the whole world had paused. Even Lala did not speak. The lamb's head tilted to the side, observing John's discomfort, but he said nothing. Prince Henry stopped mid-action, scrutinising John. Finally he broke the silence.

'Master Gavin, has this boy lost his wits?'

There was a pause before Master Gavin answered. 'I can honestly say he is a little confused, sire, but no, he is still in his right mind.'

'So, you lecture me on allowing the landless and uneducated to participate in courts when I struggle for support to extend that right to landowners. Only a madman would consider making such a move. Next you will want me including women in our government.' The prince laughed dismissively and started to turn away.

'That would not be such a bad idea.' The words slipped out, and all in the room except Prince Henry gasped. With a sinking in his stomach, the boy looked at his woolly mentor.

Sorry, I truly did not mean to say that. I do not know what came over me.

Henry swung back round and was about to speak when he was rudely interrupted.

SWAGMAN

'The boy speaks blasphemy!' The cleric who had been quietly praying in the background now rose. Shaking with suppressed anger, spittle flying from his mouth with the force of his words, he flung accusations at John. 'Seditious ideas spill from his mouth like water. Sire, you cannot allow such blasphemous words to go unpunished.'

Henry's gaze did not waver. Pinned by piercing blue eyes, John again resisted the urge to back away. Time seemed to slow down as the future king turned to the cleric.

'You are right, Friar Cedric, I cannot allow this. We are in a precarious situation at the moment. If rumours circulate I allowed a boy to discuss letting freemen and women take part in running the land, any support I gained amongst the barons will melt away like snow in the sun.

'Stanislaus, take this boy to the dungeons. Maybe a week in a cell will cool his hot head.' Prince Henry turned his back, dismissing them all.

'Sorry,' Stanislaus whispered to John as he took his arm.

Shrugging out of the loose grip, John turned to argue his point. Stanislaus shook his head, warning against such a move, and once again grabbed hold of him. This time the grip was firmer and John allowed the squire to lead him out of the hall.

Master Gavin and Lala followed behind. As they walked, John tried to think of something to do to turn this situation around. Earlier he jumped in the billabong to avoid prison, and now he was headed for something potentially worse. In his mind, dungeons were dank, dark places where people were left to rot, forgotten by everyone.

Once outside, his head and ears were bombarded with voices. Although everyone spoke over top of one another, he gleaned they all asked some variation of what he thought he was doing speaking to the future king as he would do to a man of the same station? When the noise became overwhelming, Master Gavin held up his hands to shush them.

'Boy, you do not appear to understand, the king is the ultimate power in this land. He holds life and death over us all, with little to curb his power.

'Prince Henry is progressive, but he will not tolerate having his actions questioned by a commoner. You should be grateful he only sent you to the dungeons. At least your head is still attached to your shoulders. The best we can hope for is he forgets about you, then in a bit we can petition for your release.'

'But... I meant no disrespect. I only wanted him to consider the long term effects of his actions.'

'We cannot stand about talking. If he catches us out here you might get in worse trouble. Master Gavin, you will need to take the boy's lamb as he will not be able to stay where John is going.' Stanislaus tugged on his arm, pulling him towards a doorway.

I will think about what I can do to get you out. We do not have a week to wait for Prince Henry to cool down. Lala's voice followed him. *While you are in the cold and dark, I want you to think on this—I looked into the future and if the prince did as you proposed, there would be an uprising against him within five years. His brother takes the crown and all his changes are immediately reversed.*

From that time on, the barons hold sovereignty. They

run their lands like petty fiefdoms and Briton falls into anarchy. There would not be another chance to start devolving power from the ruling classes in Briton for another 400 years.

Still, you would have stopped the shearer's strike because in your time there are no unions and non-landowners are little better off than serfs in Briton today.

Oh.

An inadequate response given the circumstances, but it was all he could manage as the heavy wooden door of the palace slammed shut behind them.

Where you come from are you able to talk to your king like you would speak to a common man?' Stanislaus asked as he led him out into the courtyard, and across the open ground towards a dark wooden door set in the base of a stone tower. Their way was lit by torches placed at intervals around the walls.

'Where I come from, the king listens to councils of both the lords of the land and the commoners,' John said. 'I foolishly assumed it would be the same here. Obviously I was wrong.'

'Yes, you were very wrong. You need to understand here in Briton the un-landed serfs are little better than cattle. They have no learning and no thoughts beyond staying alive, and they are more or less owned by their masters. What good would it be to include them in government?'

John started to argue that perhaps they would then be treated better than animals, but stopped himself. His modern ideas had placed him in trouble once already today when he spoke before thinking. Instead, he considered the other boy's words, attempting to understand them in light of his knowledge of the time.

From school he learnt non-landholding classes would not have been able to read and write. In fact, although the Queensland government passed a law saying all children between six and twelve must go to school, many of the children he knew never saw the inside of a classroom because their family's survival meant they needed to work. And, even though school was free, many families could not afford suitable clothing for their children to attend every day, so they did not go at all.

In spite of this knowledge, when he studied history at school, he always imagined medieval farmer's lives to be much the same as tenant farmers in 19th century Australia. Now he was beginning to understand he had no idea how people lived their lives outside of the castle. Maybe he should hang back a little and think about following the lead of those who knew this time better.

Sighing, he answered the squire, 'Perhaps you are right. I am tired and far from home. Everything here is so strange, I just did not think. I hope Prince Henry will forgive me my outspoken thoughts, perhaps I should go and apologise.'

He turned to head back, but his captor roughly hauled him around.

'That is the last thing you should do. Prince Henry is very annoyed with you, you need to let his temper settle awhile. Then you can apologise and hope he changes his mind about keeping you locked up.'

Another sigh escaped as they continued their journey to his prison. 'I will try to do a better job of keeping my ideas to myself.'

'Now that is a marvellous idea, a pity you did not think of it earlier,' Stanislaus responded as he pulled the heavy door open. Before entering he turned, wearing a look of sympathy on his face.

'When I came here from Normandie I found this place rather strange myself. The peasants are far rougher than at home, with much less education. I understand how odd it must be for you. I can only caution you to take some time to adjust. Until then best you learn to keep things inside. You do not want to be getting into any more trouble.'

'You come from Normandie? Where is that?' Although John asked in part to find out more about the boy, if he were honest, he also did it to delay the journey to the dungeons.

'Normandie is across the channel, in the land some call France. My father farms there, on a property given to him for his service to Sir Robert de Beaumont.'

John studied the boy as he stood in the dim torchlight. He was tall, as tall as John, which made him large for someone in medieval Briton. This he knew from the book of King Arthur his mother read. His hair was darker, and his complexion more olive than the servants here. His usual good natured demeanour changed to sadness when he talked of home.

'How did you end up here?'

'My father was a servant, but became a knight in Sir Robert's household at a young age when one of de Beaumont's men saw his potential with weapons. When he retired, he was given a grant of land for his services.

'He expected me to follow in his footsteps and learn the craft of fighting. So when Sir Robert offered to foster me in his household and treat me as a son, my father jumped at the chance. At the time I also thought the offer acceptable, although I was not asked. Sir Robert is a fair man and lives close by our family holding, so I was able to visit my parents often. Then we followed Prince Henry here.'

'Hold on. You have parents who are alive and love you, yet they sent you to live in someone else's household? That is a crazy idea.'

Stanislaus looked startled. 'You find such a practice odd? It is commonly done in Normandie, *and* here in Briton. It cements ties between the noble houses, and it is a great honour for someone as highly placed as Sir Robert to take in someone like me. Although I suspect Robert de Beaumont and my father have an understanding I shall marry Elle, the eldest Beaumont daughter, when we are old enough.'

'Did I hear you correctly? Your parents are arranging your marriage?' John was sure the strangeness of this time was confusing him and he must have misunderstood the other boy.

Smiling, Stanislaus responded, 'Where you are from must be quite different if you think such things unusual. No one of the landed class or nobility gets to choose who they marry. Everything is arranged to make strong alliances and keep power within a small group of families.'

Amazed, John blurted, 'And you are all right with them organising your life like that?' So much for keeping his opinions to himself.

'Yes, of course. It is a good match, and at least I like Elle. Many of my friends are betrothed to people they have never met.'

While Stanislaus appeared to be perfectly happy that his parents planned his future for him, would the outspoken Barabal give in as willingly to the choice made for her? His thoughts then leapt forward a few centuries, and he wondered if this age old practice was why many parents in his time still thought themselves better able to choose partners for their children?

'Anyway, it is how things are done, I try not to think too hard about it.' Stanislaus's voice penetrated his thoughts, bringing him back to the present. 'I do miss home though, and if I am being honest, I miss Elle. We grew to be close friends before I left.'

'If you miss it so much why did you come here?'

'Well, Prince Henry had a falling out with his brother Robert Curthose, Duke of Normandie, and fled to England to ask for sanctuary with his other brother, King William. Sir Robert de Beaumont is one of Prince Henry's closest friends, and he felt obliged to escort him to safety. Now de Beaumont stays because Robert Curthose is unhappy with him, and he is waiting for the duke's anger to cool before we return home.'

'That explains why de Beaumont came, but not you.'

'Sir Robert could have ordered me to come, and I would have had no choice, but he gave me the honour of making up my own mind.

'It was a hard decision for me to make. Although my father is one of Sir Robert de Beaumont's vassals, as a Norman landholder he also owes indirect fealty to Duke Robert Curthose. I spoke with my father and he said as we made a promise to serve de Beaumont faithfully, and a man is only as good as his given word, I should travel to Briton with him.'

As if Stanislaus suddenly realised they were dawdling, chatting in an open doorway, he tugged on John's arm, leading him inside.

The door opened to a candlelit stairway, going both up and down. His guard led him downwards, and John shivered as the stairs spilled them into a cold, dark corridor. Four wooden doors spaced evenly broke the stone walls, two on each side. An elderly man sat at a table placed in an alcove at the far end. He did not stop eating what looked like a watery stew until Stanislaus halted right beside him.

'We is a bit full young squire, this one will need to share, or you needs to lock him up elsewhere.'

'Prince Henry specifically asked for the dungeons. Can we put him with someone not too violent? He is a gentle soul, and I heard some real villains are held down here at the moment, horse thieves and the like.'

'We can put him in here.' The man laughed a hollow laugh. 'He might enjoy sharing with the gentleman brought in today.'

Completely missing the sarcasm, Stanislaus pushed John through the door the old man opened. 'Thank you, Tom. I will send someone down with food for him when

SWAGMAN

I can.'

'Good luck to you, John.' His parting words were almost cut off as the door slammed closed behind him.

John stood where he stumbled to a stop, allowing his eyes to adjust to the inky blackness. He could not remember ever being anywhere so dark. Even though they were below ground, the cell had a single slit of a window high up the wall. It did nothing to let in any light though as the night was black as pitch.

Something scrabbled over his foot, and he bit back a scream. Deciding he would never be able to use his eyes to find his way, he reached out and found the edge where the wooden door met the stone wall. Inch by inch, he followed his hand around until he came to where two walls met.

Concentrating on breathing in and out, he attempted to calm his nerves as he stood in the corner, legs trembling. Although the rodents scurrying around the floor made him reluctant to sit, he was so bone weary he braced himself, and slipped down the wall until his bottom hit the rush strewn floor.

Trying not to focus on the fact he was in complete darkness, in a dungeon, with things running over his legs, in a strange country eight hundred years before his birth, he attempted to control his panic. At this point, he wished he had just gone along with the militia at the billabong. Prison in his own time would have been preferable to this.

'It takes a bit of getting used to. The darkness, I mean.'

John's heart jumped into his mouth at the sound of a voice from the other side of the cell. In his terror, he forgot he shared his prison with another.

'Wha... who?' he stammered, not quite able to get a full word out.

'Sorry, did they not tell you someone else was in here already?' Bitter amusement laced the words spinning in the darkness.

'No... yes... sorry, they did. I was thrown off a bit when they closed the door. The old man said something about a gentleman being in here.'

'So, they demoted me to a mere gentleman.' Defeat now joined bitterness.

Listening to the man, John started to worry. Why would they throw a noble into the dungeons? It could only be for something unforgivable, like, maybe, murder? What sort of world was he in where a gentleman murderer was considered less dangerous than a common horse thief? A clank followed by shuffling told him the man shifted position before he spoke again.

'You are lucky they did not shackle you,' the voice said. 'At least you can move out of the way of these blasted vermin.'

John let out a sigh of relief, if he stayed on his side of the room, he would at least be safe.

'Would they put me in chains for speaking my mind to the king?' John found himself again bewildered by this place.

A harsh laugh erupted from across the way. 'Lad, people hang for less than that. Well, unless someone with power speaks up for them. Hold on a moment, we have no king. Ah, you mean Prince Henry is exercising royal prerogative. Of course he is.'

Ironically, the voice in the darkness carried more weight than Lala's admonishments. It finally dawned on John he was in dire straits. The king had absolute authority here, and although Prince Henry had not yet been crowned, he was still in absolute control. He really might lose his life for merely speaking his mind.

As the coldness seeped through his thin shirt, he wondered at how he ever thought non-landholders were hard done by in Australia in the 1890s. Compared to here, they had it much easier.

Stuck in this godforsaken hole, he finally realised the importance of these initial steps spreading the power downwards. How annoying to come to this conclusion now he was locked up and unable to help as planned. Grunting in frustration, he kicked away a rat as it attempted to nibble on his boot.

As he dwelt on his situation, he noticed the moon had risen, letting a watery light into the cell through the window. As his eyes adjusted, he could just about make out the shape of the man opposite him, leaning against the wall with his hands chained above his head.

'You must be uncomfortable.' He really needed to stop and think before opening his mouth.

'Yes, lad, more than a little. I stand and my legs ache. I sit and my arms ache. I cannot lie to sleep. I am sure though my comfort is not their main concern.'

'Why are you here? Do you mind my asking?' He added the last in case he appeared rude. His mother constantly told him off for being nosey and asking inappropriate questions.

'No, I do not mind at all. Talking helps take my mind off the pain. Besides, you may be the only person I get to tell my story to before they separate me from my head. I am accused of killing a man in cold blood.'

Frozen in place by the words, John did not know what to say next. The man he shared the dungeon with was actually a killer. Swallowing his fear, he reminded himself the other man was chained to the wall and not likely to be a threat to him. Though... he did not say he actually killed a man.

'Who do they think you killed?'

'The king, William the Second.'

'Wow.' The word escaped of its own accord. 'They did not like it when I spoke my mind to Prince Henry, I cannot imagine what they might do to you for killing a king.'

Again the other man laughed. 'Oh, they will behead me for sure. They need to ensure someone is blamed for King William's death, and I am to be the scapegoat. Just because I took the wrong track in the hunt, thinking I discovered a better trail to the deer. In the excitement, I loosed the first shot. Unfortunately, the deer moved at the last moment. The arrow sped through and hit the king, who happened to be standing behind the animal, opposite me.'

'So you are the man Prince Henry told everyone he needed to talk to about his brother's death,' John mused. 'I don't recall him talking about executing you though.'

Now the man laughed out loud. A harsh, grating laugh with no real mirth. 'You are a wet behind the ears one, truly you are. The prince has no choice but to kill me to appease the blood hounds ruling this land. When he rushed back here to get the key to the royal treasury from that bend'wi'the'wind Ranulf Flambard, he was followed by William de Breteuil.

'I had slipped back to my rooms to gather my belongings and that slimy toad de Breteuil found me. Stupid dolt! He will do anything to advance Duke Robert Curthose's suit for the crown of Briton. The man believes William the Conqueror, King William's father, made a grave mistake dividing his lands; giving his elder son the coveted barony of Normandie, and his middle son the crown of the lands he conquered in Briton.

'In the demented fool's head, de Breteuil thinks we would all be better off if the lands were again united under Robert Curthose. He believes bringing in King William's killer, and spreading rumours about my working with Prince Henry, will have the barons calling for Robert Curthose to be crowned. To be fair, I think he truly believes there was a plot to kill the king.

'One thing you can say for Henry Beauclerc though, he is smart and kept one step ahead of de Breteuil. When he turned up with me in tow, Henry thanked him for finding me, but said under his promise to the barons I would need to be accused and stand trial before all the nobles of the land. That could not happen until after the king was buried. With his clever words, he convinced the fool de Breteuil the best thing to do was to hold me here and keep quiet about my identity until after the funeral.'

For once in his life, John decided to think before he

opened his mouth. Not from politeness, but because so much information swirled round in his head he was unable to tell truth from lie. The silence lengthened, and it soon became obvious his companion waited for him to respond.

'Ah, I see,' said John, though he really did not. 'At least you will get a chance to prove you are innocent and go free when you speak before the Baron's court.'

'My young friend, you are truly naive. No, I shall be beheaded. Unlike his father, King William the Second was not well liked. Oh, he was a great soldier, in battle he was magnificent. Sadly, he bled this country dry to pay for his glory, and made many enemies along the way. They are but a few of the reasons why many think his death must have been planned.

'The fact they would have liked to kill him themselves also makes it easy for them to believe someone actually went and did it. Even so, they will turn this country upside down to find his killer. And Prince Henry needs to execute someone, lest they accuse him of plotting with the murderer.

'So here I am, having the misfortune of being in the wrong place at the wrong time, taking the fall to keep the kingdom stable. Yes, Walter Tirel will forever be known as the king's murderer, come what may.'

'But that is not fair. There has to be a trial. Surely the truth will come out.'

'I said Henry told Breteuil he would bring me before the Barons, but I am sure he will not. It is in no one's best interest for me to muddy the waters with my version of events. There were enough nobles with the king when he died to confirm the killing shot came from my bow. It will be enough for the barons to agree to my guilt. I will not even get a chance to speak.'

'That is wrong. You should not be judged by men who will gain from your conviction. They need to find someone impartial to decide what happened.' John was astounded.

'My, you do have some strange notions. I dare say if I had killed anyone but the king my family would be able to purchase a pardon, but no one has ever been pardoned for regicide.' Walter sighed and John watched as his body sagged against the wall.

'It's not right,' John said, not liking this glimpse of life in medieval Briton. It did highlight the need for Henry's proposed changes, letting leaders of the hundreds run their own courts. Although to him it first appeared to be a tiny step, he now realised what a leap forward it was. Closing his eyes, he sent a mental apology to Lala for reacting rather than thinking, and mucking up their chance to bring about change.

CHAPTER SIX
BARABAL TO THE RESCUE

As Stanislaus led John from the Great Hall, followed by Lala and Master Gavin, the men on the dais appeared to forget Barabal's existence. Unwilling to anger her future king, she did not know whether to stay or leave. No one had dismissed her, but nor were they including her in their conversation. Shifting uncomfortably from foot to foot, she waited for someone to notice her presence, while mulling over the scene she witnessed moments before.

John was a strange one. He did not understand what a great thing Henry Beauclerc proposed to do should he become king. People like her father would no longer need to go cap in hand to their baron to request justice. Even though it was still likely money not truth would win the day, men would be masters of their own destiny. They would no longer be subject to the petty whims of those who ruled by right not ability.

John appeared unaware he placed something benefitting so many in jeopardy by proposing all sorts of extreme ideas. Prince Henry would find it difficult getting the barons to agree to his proposal as things stood, if they worried about more extreme changes, he would lose the little support he had.

'God's teeth!'

Prince Henry's explosion brought her attention back to the room. The men lent over the royal coffer, the key of which dangled from Henry's hand.

'Flambard, what is the meaning of this? What is in here is scarce enough to see us through to the end of this year. I understood this quarter's taxes had been collected.'

'Well... sire, the Welsh campaign nearly emptied the coffers, and... well to put it bluntly, your brother near bled the country dry to finance your older brother's crusade.' Ranulf Flambard stumbled over his words as he fumbled for an answer that might deflect the prince's anger. 'After paying the additional tax levy King William imposed, there was little coin left for last quarter's payments. Most barons sent in promissory notes instead.

'Why else do you think King William began selling rights to church lands and livings, and taking bribes to allow some unusual marriage alliances?'

'The vain, incompetent fool. He stripped the country of its resources all for his own ends, and to have something to hold over Robert Curthose,' Prince Henry spat out through gritted teeth, his anger barely contained.

'Our first act upon coronation will be to request my

brother repay his loan. We need the money more than he does.'

'Are you sure that is wise, Henry? After all, he will not be happy at you usurping the crown he believes belongs to him. Asking for our money back will be like poking a bear with a stick. It will likely cause another war.' Robert de Beaumont counselled the future king.

'That lazy, good-for-nothing cannot keep his duchy in check, I will not allow him to destroy this country as well. Besides, he has no real claim on the throne. King William himself named me his heir. He had no queen, not even any bastard off-spring to raise to the throne. He knew he would die without a son, and he wanted me, not Curthose to rule in Briton.'

'I know, we were together when he proclaimed it, Henry. But as he did not put it in writing, Robert Curthose sees otherwise, and you know that. He, like many of the barons with Norman holdings, see Briton as a cow to be milked for their own benefit. I cannot imagine he will consider repaying the money loaned to him by King William, he will see it as his right to keep it. In fact, it is more likely he will raise an army to take the land from you. He will not let Briton go that easy.'

'By the time he stirs himself to move, the men of Briton will be united behind me. Once I am coronated, there is little he will be able to do,' Prince Henry boasted.

Frowning, Ranulf interrupted. 'If I can be so bold, sire, there are still those who prefer the idea of Robert Curthose's rule simply because he is so shiftless. They regard this as an opportunity to grasp more concessions than you are offering them.'

SWAGMAN

'Pah. A few men. Most support me now I have offered them some relief from their monetary problems.' The prince dismissed the idea.

'A few men, yes, but a dangerous few. I would not turn my back on them, de Breteuil especially,' Ranulf warned.

Closing the chest Prince Henry turned and caught sight of Barabal still waiting nearby.

'Is there something else, Mistress Barabal?'

Face turning red under the Prince's scrutiny, Barabal had never wished more to be able to control her blushing.

'Umm, begging pardon, sire, but I have not been dismissed.'

The prince frowned, and Barabal thought he would explode again. Instead he burst out laughing.

'Why, you are correct. That was remiss of me. I am sure I need not remind you what you heard here is private, and not to be discussed with the other servants.'

'Barabal was my wife's maid for two years, and we have always found her trustworthy,' Ranulf informed them.

'She has been looking after my wife since we arrived in Briton, and we trust her implicitly,' Robert de Beaumont added his support. 'In fact, I believe my wife asked her to return to Normandie with us.'

While Barabal felt a rush of gratitude for their kind words, she did not have the heart to tell de Beaumont she did not want to go with him and his family to a foreign land.

Prince Henry regarded her intently for a moment, then smiled. It was like a cloud had passed overhead and the sun suddenly reappeared.

'It is good you stayed behind. I need a letter taken to

Princess Edith tomorrow, and you shall deliver it for me.'

Barabal frowned, wondering how she might be able to take advantage of the situation she found herself in.

'Is there a problem?' Prince Henry pursed his lips. 'Well, speak up, girl.'

'I cannot go alone, sire, I would need Stanislaus and John to accompany me for protection, and to help me into the Abbey without being seen. It is important to go undetected because people would comment if I were to meet with Princess Edith twice in two days. I am sure you would not like rumours to spread.'

'Take Stanislaus by all means,' Robert de Beaumont told her, releasing his squire from his normal duties. 'But who is this John? Is he one of the Winchester guards?'

'The boy Prince Henry sent to the dungeons,' Barabal spoke quickly, hoping to gloss over the incident and have her master and the prince agree to John's presence without thinking too much about it. Her ploy was unsuccessful, Robert de Beaumont was far too shrewd to be taken in that easily.

'Take Alain with you by all means, if Master Gavin can spare him. That other boy stays where he is. He needs to learn to keep to his place.' Prince Henry commanded.

'Begging you pardon, sire, perhaps one night in the dungeons is punishment enough for such a misstep. He is not from around here and intended no real harm.'

'Barabal,' de Beaumont whispered. 'You worry for your new friend, but you must not harry Prince Henry on this. Leave things a couple of days and I will see what I can do for him.'

'Come to me in the morning at first light and I will

have a letter ready for you.' Prince Henry turned away, the matter decided, and walked towards the private quarters at the back of the hall.

Barabal resisted the urge to stamp her foot in frustration, certain had she been a boy Prince Henry would have paid more attention to her request to release John. Her anger must have shown on her face as Robert de Beaumont stepped between her and the retreating prince.

'Go and eat some supper, then return to your mistress. We will talk about this later.'

Curtseying, Barabal backed away, annoyed her efforts to free John had been in vain. Well, there was more than one way to skin an apple. Foregoing supper, she decided to find Alain.

Waiting in the shadows outside Master Gavin's rooms, Barabal formulated a plan to rescue John from his prison. All she needed now was to persuade Alain and Stanislaus to work with her. She knew she could twist Stanislaus round her little finger. Since she moved to Sir Robert de Beaumont's household they had become fast friends. However, for her plan to work, she needed Alain's help, and the other boy was an unknown quantity.

Since King William's court moved to Winchester less than a month ago, Stanislaus spent most of his spare time with Alain. Barabal only knew the apothecary's apprentice through the squire. Talking to him first was a risk, but without him her plan would have no chance of succeeding.

Her patience paid off, the door opened and Master Gavin emerged, followed by his apprentice. Deep in conversation, the master walked by the hiding place without even noticing her. As Alain passed, she reached out and touched his sleeve, putting the finger of her other hand to her lips. Jerking her head to the side, indicating the door behind, Barabal hoped he understood she wanted to talk to him in private. Fortunately the boy's serious green eyes flickered with understanding.

Catching up with the apothecary he said, 'Master Gavin, sorry, I forgot I did not properly store the elixir I worked on earlier. In all the excitement I left the stoppers off while it cooled and forgot to put them on later. I will go back, finish the job, then catch you up.'

'It could wait until after we ate, but I guess with that lamb frolicking around we do not want to risk an accident. I will meet you in the hall.' Master Gavin carried on, not wishing to delay his evening meal waiting for his apprentice.

Letting out the breath she held, Barabal followed Alain back into the apothecary's rooms, and waited until he closed the door behind them before speaking.

'Alain, I need your help. Stanislaus said something today. Do you... do you know how to blow something up?'

She rushed the words out, having previously decided a direct approach appealing to the boy's sense of adventure was the best way to attack the problem. Alain frowned at her and ran his hand through his curly midnight black hair while he considered his answer.

'Master Gavin and I have been experimenting with a little Greek fire he managed to buy from some pedlars,' he finally admitted. 'Why?'

How annoying, she grumbled. Used to dealing with loyal, steadfast Stanislaus who never thought to question her, she found this boy's curiosity irritating and time wasting. She chose to ignore his question.

'Would you be able to use it to, say, open a locked door?' She arranged her face to appear honest and as if she was a little in awe of Alain. This approach usually resulted in boys eating out of her hand, but not with this one. His frown deepened and she detected distrust in his eyes.

'I will tell you no more until you tell me why you want to know.' Crossing his arms firmly across his chest, his gazed bored into her.

Barabal glared straight back, not intimidated by Alain in the least. Realising she had no other option, she shrugged her shoulders.

'All right. I want your help to break a boy out of the dungeons.'

'Do you have a plan?'

Barabal's eyes widened. She expected allegations of madness or worries about getting caught, but not this matter-of-fact question.

Alain chuckled at her discomfort, took her by the arm, and led her to the table. After she was seated, he picked up John's lamb from in front of the fire and placed the animal in his lap as he sat opposite her.

'Before going to dinner we spent time discussing this very problem,' Alain continued speaking once he was settled. 'But we were unable to think of a way to rescue John without Henry Beauclerc being able to trace it back to us.

We thought something to eat may help fuel our brains, which was what we were going to do when I met you.'

Barabal smiled a genuine smile this time, pleased she no longer needed to play the simpering girl to get what she wanted.

'I think I may be able to help you. My plan means we can get away without being found out... hopefully.'

'Go ahead then.' Alain nodded encouragingly, and Barabal looked down to find the lamb watching her. If she did not know better, she would have sworn he too was listening.

'Prince Henry asked me to go to Romsey Abbey tomorrow morning to take a letter. You and Stanislaus are to come with me. I think if we time this right, I can pick up the letter, we can start on our way, then you two can double back, blow the lock on John's door and bring him along with us. That way no one will suspect any of us of helping him escape.'

Alain looked into the distance for a moment, then asked, 'What about the guard? How will we get past him?'

'You will not need to.' Barabal grinned, impressed by her own brilliance. 'I am sure you have observed the day guard is sweet on one of the kitchen maids.'

Alain's puzzled face told her he had not.

'Really, you have not seen how he follows her around with puppy dog eyes?'

Again nothing, and Barabal suppressed her sigh. She was constantly amazed men ever got anywhere in life as they did not seem to pick up on any of the little things happening around them. Consequently, they had no idea how such things might be used to their benefit.

SWAGMAN

'Anyway, he often brings his breakfast plate back to the kitchen, and lingers to talk with her. He normally stays about five to ten minutes, and returns via the privy.

'If we hold our departure until we see the guard take is plate to the kitchen, once we are out of sight, you boys can double back. You would have about ten or fifteen minutes to blow the door and fetch John, that is, if you slip in as the guard leaves.'

'That might work.' Alain drew his words out as if he were still thinking things through. 'The only problem might be the Greek fire. We are still experimenting with it. To say Greek fire is unpredictable is an understatement. A small amount might blow the lock, or it might take down half the building.'

'But worth a try?' Barabal asked impatiently.

A slow smile spread across his face as he seemed to check with the lamb on his lap, who looked as though he was nodding in agreement.

'Yes, we should definitely give it a try. Let us find Stanislaus and tell him what he needs to do.'

'Do you not mean ask him?' Barabal countered.

'I am sure you worked out long ago, things go more smoothly if you do not let Stan think too much about his role in a plan.'

Barabal laughed, realising she liked this boy. He was not threatened by how smart she was, and he treated her as an equal. A rare quality in her experience.

CHAPTER SEVEN
PRISON BREAK

John changed position yet again. If he sat for too long his bottom hurt. If he stood, his legs soon grew tired. If he lay down, well he only tried that once—the rats swarmed over him. Now completely exhausted, still sleep would not come. Kicking his leg out, he dislodged yet another rodent before leaning back against the wall in the hopes he might find some comfort.

With his stomach growling his hunger, he tried to think of something, anything else other than food. Last night, sure Stanislaus would not forget his promise to send something to eat, he asked Walter when to expect supper. The man barked out yet another of his bitter laughs before answering.

'Sorry, lad, they will not waste food on those who are not long for this earth.'

SWAGMAN

That had not comforted him at all. After a restless night he continued to worry about whether or not they might still decide to kill him. He answered his own question. Yes, they might. In this time and place where one man made the laws, and where a person without land was little better than an animal, no one would stop Prince Henry doing whatever he wanted with him.

Sighing, John stood and stretched his limbs, wishing whatever they were going to do with him they would just get on with it and put him out of his misery. If they waited too long, these blasted rats would ensure there was nothing left of him to punish.

Reaching his arms up to stretch his back, John was thrown forward, almost losing his footing, then pushed backwards, slamming into the wall and ending up flat on his bottom, narrowly avoiding banging his head against the stone floor. An acrid smell filled the air. As his eyesight adjusted to the influx of light, he found the cell door now lying in pieces on the rushes.

'I think you used a little too much of the Greek fire.'

'Do you think?' A sarcastic voice responded.

Either the blast had damaged his ears, or Stanislaus was breaking him out.

Expecting his friend, John was bemused to find himself face to face with someone he had never seen before. The stranger studied the scene in front of him and finally fixed his gaze on Walter.

'Stan, did you not think it important to tell me he shared a cell with someone?'

Entering the room, Stanislaus' face split into a wide grin when his eyes found John. 'Oh, I forgot. When I brought him down it was a bit full so they put John in with someone else.'

'Dolt. Now we have to deal with a witness.' Frowning, the boy looked directly at John. 'Come on then. Don't just sit there, we are rescuing you.'

'What you mean "deal with him"?' Stanislaus asked, then his eyes widened in alarm. 'You do not mean kill him, do you? I am not sure I could do that.'

John rose to his feet while Stanislaus and the other boy discussed what to do with the man chained to the wall.

'Set him free.' John offered his opinion as he joined them in the still smoking doorway.

'What?' In unison the two boys turned and gaped at him.

'Has a night down here sent you even more mad? Who knows what he has done? It must be something violent, he is chained to a wall,' the unfamiliar boy said.

'According to him he did nothing, but they think he killed the king. Anyway, it does not matter what he did, you are both in danger if he tells anyone who rescued me.'

Ignoring Stanislaus' muttering, the boy stared at the ceiling as if the solution would appear before him, then spoke to John. 'What a brilliant idea. If we release him, they will think all of this was for his benefit. I mean, who would go to all this trouble to rescue a mere boy? No one will ever suspect us of being involved.'

'What?' Stanislaus shook his head in confusion. 'Alain, you mean to set King William Rufus' killer free? If they capture him and he tells them about us, we will swing for sure.'

'But you will run like the wind, will you not?' the other

boy, Alain, asked Walter as he fiddled for something in his pocket. 'Ah, here we are.' He pulled out a thin piece of metal and set to work freeing the noble from his chains.

'I have friends nearby, in Southampton, who will smuggle me out of the country. Briton will never see my face again.'

Walter Tirel forced himself upright and, before Stanislaus found his voice to object, he ran out the door, his footsteps echoing along the corridor as he escaped his prison.

'Look what you have done,' said Stanislaus in dismay. 'We only planned to help John. Now we will really be in trouble.'

'Only if they catch us.' Alain seemed to be relishing his adventure. 'Come now,' he grabbed John by the shirt and started pulling him towards the door. 'We must be gone before the guard returns.'

John followed him out. He stopped when he realised Stanislaus still stood in the middle of the cell, mouth hanging open as he tried to comprehend the enormity of what he had just been a part of.

'Stan. Stanislaus! Come on.' Alain urged him from the hallway. 'If you stand in the cell like a dolt you will get caught.'

As if in a daze, the squire turned and, dragging his feet with reluctance, left the dungeon. John and Stanislaus were still on the stairs when Alain stepped through the door into the courtyard, then immediately ducked back inside, forcing John to stumble back into Stanislaus.

'Up,' the boy said, darting up the winding stairway. The others followed, only stopping when the shadows hid them from anyone coming through the doorway below.

Seconds later, a whistled tune drifted up to them as someone opened the external door and headed downstairs. Stanislaus went to move, but Alain held his hand up, signalling for them to wait. A moment later the whistling stopped, and curses John had never heard before filled the air. A crash and a shudder as the door banged against the outside wall proceeded the announcement of their escape.

'Help! Prisoner escape. Ring the bells.'

'Now.'

Alain led the two other boys down the stairs and through the open door. Crouching close to the ground, they managed to make it behind a wagon unloading barrels before the courtyard erupted with the sound of thundering feet and clanging metal. All other activity in the castle precinct ceased as everyone turned to the dungeons.

Holding his finger to his lips, Alain stuck his head out, attempting to gain a better view of the frantic activity. John searched for a better hiding place. Tapping Alain on the shoulder, he pointed to a gap under a lean-to close by. Alain nodded, then frowned as a man in the prince's colours wandered over to stand by the opening. As he watched the mayhem around him, he leaned against the wall, idly picking food from his teeth.

'Stanislaus, you need to go over and distract that man so we can hide properly. Then go and find Barabal and tell her the bad news. Tell her we will meet her when we are able.'

'But surely they will not think you or I are involved in this,' Stanislaus said, a worried frown creasing his brow.

SWAGMAN

'No, they probably will not. However, if we all stroll out of here someone might recognise John, and then all our good work will be for nothing.'

Stanislaus thought for a moment then, without even acknowledging his friends' words, he crawled backwards until he was able to stand without it being obvious he had been hiding. He sauntered across to the guard as if he had not a care in the world, and struck up a conversation. Moving around so the man had to turn to face him, the guard's back was now to the wagon allowing the boys to move without being seen.

'That is what I love about Stanislaus. Ask him to protect someone and he will do so without a thought for his own safety.' Alain's voice filled with pride for his friend.

'It is unlikely anyone will worry about trying to find you with Tirel on the loose, but we cannot be too careful. Prince Henry has a mind for detail and we cannot assume he will not remember you and wonder where you are.

'Are you ready? We will need to be quick and quiet. No, wait.'

The other boy sank back down and John caught a brief glimpse of Henry Beauclerc as he exited the palace, his face a picture of rage. Catching sight of Stanislaus in conversation with one of his men, he turned beetroot red and strode over to the pair.

'What are you two doing standing gawping? Stanislaus, you are meant to be with Barabal, off with you now. And, you there, whatever your name is, prisoners have escaped. You should be searching for them, not standing around chatting.' Striding off to the dungeons, the future king did not wait around to see his orders obeyed.

Stanislaus risked a quick glimpse towards the wagon before heading off to find Barabal, and the guard marched behind the prince to the dungeons. As they disappeared from view, Alain tapped John on the shoulder and pointed to the lean-to. From where they crouched, they could just make out a depression in the dirt allowing access to a hiding place underneath.

'Run fast, keep low. I will make sure no one sees you.'

John shuffled passed the other boy, glanced around to make sure no one was watching, then made a crouching run for the dark space. As he neared the hole, he slid along the ground, reaching above to grab hold of a board to pull himself fully underneath. Taking a deep breath, he wriggled back to make enough room for Alain.

His heart raced and he tried to take deep breaths to slow it down, and to minimise the sound of blood pounding in his ears. It was so loud it drowned out everything else, preventing him from hearing what was happening outside.

'Alain. Alain, what are you doing sneaking around behind that cart? Trying to find out what is going on, no doubt. Are you not supposed to be going with Barabal and Stanislaus to deliver that message for Prince Henry?'

The unfamiliar voice had John inching forward until he had a clear view of the courtyard, just in time to catch Alain standing up and dusting himself off. From his hiding place all John was able to make out was the voice belong to someone wearing the leggings of a noble.

'Sir Ranulf, please do not say anything to the prince. Nothing ever happens here in Winchester. Now, with the prison break, it was so exciting I could not help myself.

'Barabal is perfectly safe with Stanislaus protecting

her, in fact I am not sure why they asked me to go with her in the first place. I am pretty useless with a sword. Do you know what happened?'

John marvelled at how calmly Alain moved from conspirator to the role of young boy attempting to justify his skiving.

'Nothing for you to concern yourself with,' Sir Ranulf told him. 'You had best be on your way. Although you may think Barabal safe with one escort, Prince Henry specifically asked for you to accompany her. With the mood this will put him in, you would not like to be found disobeying his orders.'

'But...'

'No *buts,* you young scallywag, this is not the time for one of your pranks, or any high-jinx. Be off with you.'

'Yes, sir. My travel things are in my room. I will collect them and go find her immediately.'

'Be quick about it, and make sure you are gone before Henry leaves that dungeon. If he finds out you are still here, even my support will not save you from his wrath.'

The legs of the nobleman walked towards the dungeon door and, when he was far enough away not to hear, Alain whispered loudly, 'Wait here for me, I will come back for you in a moment.'

Once again John was left in a cold dark place, but not quite as alone as he thought. A rodent scrabbled over his leg and he suppressed a shiver.

The boards above John's head creaked and two legs dropped down in front of the hole.

'Psst, pull this on,' Alain shoved something through the gap.

'A skirt?' John questioned as he attempted to make out what the other boy had given him.

'Yes, and do not dally, it is getting busy out here.' Stifling his chuckles at John's discomfort, Alain continued, 'Once you are done, slide out. I will try and keep you covered, or at least distract anyone who shows an interest in what we are doing.'

John struggled in the confined space to pull the woollen skirt over his boots and trousers. With Alain's foot tapping impatiently, he fumbled with the unfamiliar article of clothing. *How do girls manage with this?* John thought as he tried to wriggle the skirt on over his hips, getting his feet tangled in the fabric in the process.

'Hurry up.' Alain's strained tones reached him.

'I am going as fast as I can. Wait a minute, nearly there.' John told him as his head popped out of the hole.

Alain jumped to his feet in a flash, a cloak held out for John to wrap himself in. It was huge. The original owner was around John's height, but more than three times his size. The shorter boy choked back a laugh as he tugged the hood up over John's head. Pulling himself together, he issued instructions.

'Do not speak. Follow a few paces behind me, and try to behave like you just happen to be going the same way I am.' Passing him a basket with a few items in it, Alain explained, 'Put this over your arm and you should look like any goodwife going about her daily business.'

SWAGMAN

'Goodwife,' John spluttered. 'You are helping me escape by dressing me as a woman? Great!'

Closing his eyes to block out his embarrassment, he could only imagine what the men in the shearing shed would say if they ever heard about this. They would start calling him Matilda, and asking to snuggle up with him at night. Unable to stop his face flushing red with the image, he pulled the hood down lower, hiding in its folds.

'I cannot do this.' His mouth was dry with fear.

'If you want to get out of here with your head still attached, you need to try.' Alain was all seriousness now.

John gulped and said begrudgingly, 'All right. Lead on.' After all, what other choice did he have?

Alain turned and started off out of the castle bailey. Waiting a few moments, John followed, trying really hard to take smaller steps. He crouched down to appear elderly, hoping old age might explain his strange gait. It took all his concentration to make sure he did not trip over the skirt, so he did not realise they had left the castle precinct and entered the town until he bumped into Alain. Along with everyone else on the street, the boy had stopped suddenly.

Gazing from under his hood, John glimpsed a group of guards heading down the muddy street towards them. His stomach lurched. Had they found him already? Hoping to hide in the crowd, he joined the others moving to the side of the road making way for the guards. Staring at the ground, he tried to ignore the boots coming to a stop in front of him. All he could hear was a pounding in his head. His heart beat so fast he thought it might explode.

'Alain, there you are. Barabal and Stanislaus are

waiting at the gates for you. Best hurry along or they will leave you behind.'

'I got held up in all the ruckus, I am on my way to meet them now.' Alain's voice rose above the general mutterings. 'Should I try slipping past the guards? Or should I wait until they pass by?'

'I would wait if I were you as we have some of Prince Henry's men with us. One of them may see you moving about and, not knowing who you are, might think you are hiding something. If you are detained for questioning, Barabal will be even more unhappy.' The owner of the boots laughed, as if sharing a secret with Alain. 'And I would not like her to take her anger out on me, or you for that matter.'

'Thank you,' Alain said to the retreating soldier.

John steadied his hands and took a couple of deep breaths to still his nerves. That was a little too close for him. He sensed rather than saw Alain continue up the street towards the town walls. Lifting his head slightly to keep the other boy's back in view, John followed.

Hampered by his skirts and long cloak, he was unable to slip between people the same way Alain could, and he soon lost sight of his rescuer.

Had he turned off? No, the side streets were empty. Trying hard not to panic, he approached the city walls. The gate was guarded, but they were not stopping everyone, just the few they thought suspicious. John prayed like he had never prayed before.

Attempting to blend in with the people leaving Winchester, he drew level with the guards. As he did, Alain appeared from no where and sidled up to the soldier closest to John.

SWAGMAN

'Good morrow, Bran, I am supposed to meet Mistress Barabal by the gate this morning, but she is not here. Have you seen her?'

'Yes, and she is very unhappy. First Stanislaus was late meeting her, now they are both waiting for you. I guess you were delayed by the searches.'

'That I was, but if I am being totally honest, I did dally a little. There may never be another escape from the dungeons so I did not want to miss this one. I do not think Barabal needs to know that.' John overheard Alain as he passed through the town gate, and he imagined the boy's conspiratorial wink. 'I guess I had better go find her. Do you know where she is, by the way?'

'Yes, follow the path to the left. The cart is waiting on the road to Romsey. Do not delay any longer, you do not want to make her madder than she is.'

Overhearing the instructions as he was sure Alain intended, John turned left once through the gate. He followed the path around the walls as if he planned to go that way all along. A quick glance showed him a cart with two people waiting beside the dirt track everyone here called a road, parked near a conveniently placed hedge.

Ignoring Barabal and Stanislaus, he followed the shrubbery along past the horse and cart. When he found a gap, he took the opportunity to duck in behind the hedge, having first checked no one was nearby. Taking off the skirt and cloak he bundled them up and made sure they were well hidden under the hedgerow.

He did not have to wait long before the clip of a horse's hooves announced his ride was leaving. As the cart passed his hiding place he nipped out from behind the bushes. Making sure he kept the wagon between him and the castle, he rolled on to the back tray, slipping under a canvas cover, and waited for the shout telling him he had been spotted. When none came, he breathed freely again.

CHAPTER EIGHT
TO ROMSEY ABBEY

Once the walls of Winchester were behind them, the cart slowed and Stanislaus came round back to let John out from his hiding place. In the light, the boy found he shared the cart with his pack, bedroll and, of course, Lala. He found the sleeping lamb curled up on a bundle of clothes.

'Not another dress,' John groaned and Stanislaus laughed.

'No. We thought it was time you changed from those strange garments you wear into something more local.'

Tipping Lala off his bed, Stanislaus handed the bundle to John, and pointed to a copse of trees close by.

Holding up the clothes, John was not convinced he would not be better off dressing as a woman. They expected him to exchange his trousers and shirt for what, in essence, were a long shirt and woollen leggings. The leggings appeared to be held in place with a draw string tie and bits of cloth criss-crossed up his calves. A leather belt would draw the shirt in a little at the waist and prevent it from flapping up.

'Are you sure you want me to wear this? My own clothes are more practical, and comfortable too, I am sure.'

Barabal turned around, brow creased in displeasure. 'We just went to a lot of trouble to rescue you, I do not want all our good work undone because you stand out dressed the way you are. Now, go get changed and be quick about it. We are already late starting out.'

Stanislaus wiggled his eyebrows and wrinkled his nose as Barabal turned back around, causing the other boys to laugh.

'It is all right for you,' John told him. 'You at least get to dress as a fighting man. I will be dressing like a...' he could not find the words to complete his sentence.

'Like me, you mean,' Alain asked. 'I may not be able to wield a sword, but I was the one who actually rescued you, so do you think now is the best time to make fun of the way I dress?'

Sighing, John knew when he was beaten. He mentally threw daggers at the strangely quiet Lala, before wandering over to the trees to change. Taking off his shirt and rolling down his under clothes, he started to pull the woollen tunic on. He shuddered as the coarse, scratchy fabric brushed against his skin. Deciding he would keep his long-johns on for comfort's sake, he removed the shirt and pulled his under clothes back up before continuing to dress.

A few minutes later he returned to the cart, wearing his new clothes and feeling like a bit of a fool. Stanislaus handed him a pair of soft leather boots, no where near as sturdy as his own. Outfit complete, he rolled his own clothes up and tucked them inside his pack, along with his boots. His mother would skin him alive if he turned up back home minus his clothing and footwear. That was if he ever made it back there.

I hope you are happy now, he said to Lala. *I must look like a right odd-ball.*

The lamb stared back at him with unblinking black eyes. John wondered briefly if his companions somehow managed to mix his lamb up with another. Then a tingling sensation pierced his head.

Sorry, it took a lot out of me, enabling you to understand the language while you were not in my presence. I am sure you do not need me to tell you, no matter how uncomfortable you are, you at least fit in, Lala said as he curled up on top of John's pack.

'Are you ready yet?' Barabal asked without turning, her tart tone indicating she was still unhappy with him.

'I guess so.' John mumbled as he hauled himself up, leaning back against the side of the cart.

Stanislaus glanced over his shoulder to check he was settled, then immediately swung back around, eyes round with surprise.

'Has your hair grown?'

John reached up to find his hair, which had been getting a little long and straggly, was now well down below his ears. Frowning he wondered how his hair managed to grow so much overnight. Wearily, his gaze moved to the lamb as he answered the boy.

'Ah, no,' he stuttered. 'It is the same length it was

before, I have not had time to comb it today.'

Satisfied with his answer, the squire started them back on their journey. Losing his balance as the cart lurched forward, John righted himself and fixed his gaze back on the lamb.

Lala, what did you do?

The lamb opened a single eye, *I may have contributed a little to your disguise by helping your hair grow. Quit complaining. If you had not opened your mouth without thinking, you would not need a disguise. If you do not like it, think of it as your punishment.*

Annoyed, but unable to come up with anything else to say to the guardian, he instead turned his attention to more immediate matters.

'How long is it to where we are going?'

Alain answered, 'Romsey Abbey. From Winchester to there is about sixteen miles, so we should arrive late afternoon, if all goes to plan.'

'We would have completed our task and been on our way back if you boys had not wasted so much time this morning,' Barabal interrupted acerbically.

'We would not have taken so long if Stanislaus had informed us our prisoner had a cellmate, before we blew the door down,' Alain's tone sounded annoyed to John's ear.

'Maybe next time if you two think to include me in your planning I might remember to pass on all the important details,' Stanislaus added good-naturedly. 'Besides, we are all here now, can we not just enjoy the ride?'

'Thank you for getting me out of there.' John belatedly voiced his appreciation. Until now there had been no time to show the three of them his gratitude for ensuring he escaped captivity with his head still attached.

'We could not just leave you there. Who knows how long you would have been kept in that cell before someone remembered to let you out.' Barabal shifted on her seat so she could see him. 'Besides, I feel responsible for you, having saved your life yesterday. But please do not do anything that stupid again.'

'I won't,' John assured her. 'A night in the dungeon taught me to keep my mouth shut.'

Really?

Yes, really. John blushed. *I am sorry, but I did not realise how much of a change Henry Beauclerc was proposing yesterday. A night in the dungeons really did open my eyes.*

Compared to the time you live in, it must seem so very little, Lala conceded, not wasting energy to even raise his head as he mind-spoke.

I had a long conversation with my cell mate last night. I came to realise most people have so few rights here a court in the hundreds would be an enormous change.

Silence followed his revelation, and John checked to make sure Lala had not gone to sleep. The lamb raised his eyes and met John's gaze.

It is possible I made a mistake bringing you straight to the castle. If we wandered through the countryside a little first you may have been better prepared for what you need to do. I will take that into account on my second mission.

Second mission? Is this your first time doing this?

No. Well, sort of. Of course I went out with masters to assist, but yes, this is my first time solo, the lamb eventually admitted.

Great. I am hundreds of years in the past, in a strange country, expected to ensure certain events occur so history can evolve without a hitch; and my guide is a lamb who is on his first mission. Could this get any better?

It could be worse, you could still be locked in a cell. Lala snorted and repositioned himself, back to John, showing exactly what he thought of his comments.

With the sun directly overhead, Barabal stopped them for a noontime snack. John blushed as he realised he had eaten a large portion of the food while the others looked on in astonishment. After he emptied his mouth, he explained he had not eaten since midday the day before. Embarrassed at forgetting to bring him food the previous evening, Stanislaus reached into the food basket and handed him another leg of chicken.

'I was saving this for later, but you need it more than me. To say sorry for last night.'

John was touched by the other boy's generosity.

Back in the cart, having not slept much the night before, he soon found the gentle rocking motion caused his eyelids to droop. Lying down, he followed fluffy clouds drifting slowly across the azure blue sky.

'John. JOHN. We are here.' Alain shook his shoulder none too gently.

Lift me down.

Blearily looking around, he found the cart parked by a stone wall. The crisp lines between the stones, and the lack of moss, indicated the wall had recently been erected. Sighing, he sat up to get his bearings, jerking at a cold nose on his hand. Glancing down, he saw Lala standing beside him expectantly. Without thinking, he picked the lamb up and placed him on the ground. Lala promptly wandered to the grass verge and relieved himself.

Some water if you please.

Once again John automatically did as he was bid, putting some water in a pottery bowl he found in the back by the food basket. He grabbed a mug and filled it for himself from the water skin. The cool, fresh water contained none of the underlying hints of mud he was used to. Thirst quenched, the lamb wandered away and delicately nibbled on the grass.

'If you have quite finished...' Barabal stood in front of him, hand on hips covering his legs in shadows. 'We must get ready to go inside. We need to talk to Princess Edith before vespers.'

'Why? And what is vespers.' John asked, still not quite awake enough to deal with the oddities of this place.

'Vespers is evensong service, and there is no talking in the nunnery afterwards. If we do not conclude our business before then, we will need to wait until tomorrow.' The girl moved to the side inviting him to get down.

'Are we climbing over the wall?' John stared doubtfully at the structure beside him. 'It must be at least ten feet high.'

Barabal laughed, 'And give you boys a chance to look up my skirts? No, I have a better idea.'

Walking around the cart, Barabal reached over and opened what John had assumed was another basket of food. The lid dropped back to reveal swathes of black cloth. Pulling out the item on top and shaking it out, her plan became clear.

'No,' he sighed. 'I am not dressing up in skirts again. Once a day is enough for any red-blooded boy.'

Barabal stared balefully at him. 'Do not make me wish we left you behind.'

'I am happy to climb the wall if you need me to,' John volunteered.

'I would like you to tell me how you think you will be able to move around a Benedictine Convent dressed as a man.'

John's mouth formed an „O". 'When you said our destination was Romsey Abbey, I thought you meant a church.'

Barabal frowned. 'How can you not know that Romsey Abbey is a convent? Daughters of kings and nobles come from far away lands to study here. This particular convent is famous in all the known world as a place to educate young women. Even if you are not from close by, you should still have heard of the abbey.'

'Leave him alone, Barabal. Just because you always dreamt of being asked to attend the school here does not mean everyone else has heard of it.'

Stanislaus finished tying the horses to the stakes he and Alain had driven into the ground by the edge of the forest, and came to take the habit Barabal held out for him. Picking up another from the basket, he and Alain nipped behind some trees to change.

'You want to go here?' John asked.

'I want to learn more than how to write and do household

accounts,' Barabal answered, a touch of sadness tinging her words. 'I want to read the writings of great thinkers and learn how the world works. However, although my father owns his own land, he could never afford the endowment for me to attend the Abbey.'

'Endowment?'

'Yes, to be educated here you must pay a fee. That enables the abbess and the sisters to teach rather than having to farm the land for their survival.'

'Oh. So if you are a girl the only way you can learn is to join a convent and take holy vows?'

If this was the case, he decided his mother's book on medieval knights had been sadly lacking in real information.

'No, silly, you are not expected to become a nun. Though you are required to live in the convent and follow their rules while you study here.'

Shrugging her shoulders, Barabal smiled, forcing the sadness from her eyes as her usual optimism returned.

'Come now, you must get dressed, we have not got much time here if we are to catch Prince Henry up on the road to London tomorrow.'

'London? We are going to London?'

She reached into the basket and pulled out some more black cloth.

'Yes, Prince Henry is taking the court there so he can be crowned in the great abbey. When we are done, we are to join him and attend the coronation.' Handing him the garments she turned her back to give him privacy and at the same time telling him, 'You do not need to take your clothes off, just pull this on over top.'

He dressed as per her instructions, as he did he asked,

'Do you think it wise for me to meet up with Henry? You know, since I escaped from his dungeon.'

Barabal snorted. 'There will be so many people travelling with the royal party we will be able to keep you well enough hidden. We can keep you dressed as a nun if it would make you any happier.'

'I think maybe I would rather stay here.'

Barabal turned to hand him the piece of black cloth. 'Your wimple,' she advised.

'Wimple? What...' John inspected the cloth as if it was some strange piece of equipment he needed to figure out.

'Here let me. You need to bend down,' she directed, taking the wimple from his hands. As he bent, she placed the cloth over his head like some kind of veil. It fell over his shoulders and down his front, hiding his hair and obscuring his face.

Barabal inspected him. 'I guess that will do. Best you keep your head down, like you are praying,' she said as she held up some rosary beads. 'Do you at least know how to use these?'

John nodded, thankful his best friend at school had been catholic and told him once the beads on the rosary were used to count the number of times you said a prayer.

'Good. You fix them like this.' Barabal reached around him and tied the beads like a belt, with the cross hanging down just above his knees. Job done, she turned towards the trees.

'Come on, you two, we have not got all day. It will be dark soon and we will be caught inside the walls for the night if we do not hurry.'

'Are you not getting changed too?' John asked as they

waited for Stanislaus and Alain to appear.

'No, silly, women visitors are commonplace here.'

Her face crumpled into a frown as the other boys appeared from behind the bushes. She marched over and made them stand still while she adjusted their costumes to her satisfaction. Once they were dressed appropriately, she lined them up. With John walking beside her, and Alain and Stanislaus following behind, they were ready to go.

Walking around the wall, John spied a closed gate. It did not appear very inviting, yet Barabal strode over and thumped authoritatively on the wood. A small metal peep-hole opened and a face peered out.

'We are here to see Princess Edith.'

Without any verbal response, the door opened to admit the strange group.

'She is where you usually find her,' a female voice came from behind the wooden barrier.

Barabal nodded, and confidently strode ahead towards a side entrance in one of the stone buildings. John turned to catch a glimpse of the woman closing the gate behind them ,and was surprised to see Lala following Alain.

Lala, what are you doing?

Do you think I trust you alone after yesterday? the lamb asked.

A lamb cannot just go wandering about in a convent, John told him.

I think you will find that I am more welcome here than you would be if they found out you were a boy, the lamb chuckled as they reached the side door.

CHAPTER NINE
MEETING THE REAL MATILDA

John kept his eyes on the polished wooden floor as Barabal led them through a hallway lined on both sides with closed doors.

'The sister's rooms.'

Although she whispered, Barabal's voice echoed alarmingly in the empty corridor. She huddled them close so she could keep the noise to a minimum before continuing.

'The library, where Princess Edith will be, is through the main vestibule and at the end of a corridor on the other side. Please do not gawp as we go through the entranceway, I do not want you doing anything to draw attention to yourselves. Things will go easier for us if we pass unnoticed.'

No one said anything in response as they returned to

their earlier formation. Turning the corner, they proceeded down another door lined hall that soon opened into a larger area. Not wishing a repeat of the night before, John kept his head down as instructed until a commanding voice halted their party.

'You. Yes, you. What do you think you are doing?'

Reacting as though she spoke to him, John lifted his eyes to see a woman dressed all in black, wearing the most ornate cross imaginable around her neck. Idly wondering if the jewels were real, he dropped his head and waited for Barabal to speak for them.

The green of her dress pooled around her feet as she curtseyed. 'Good evening, Reverend Mother. These sisters are escorting me to visit with your niece. I believe she is in the library.'

'I guess you bring with you another message from that young man.'

Her lips pursed as if she was sucking a lemon, making it obvious Princess Edith's suitor did not come high on her list of suitable husbands. John was just able to see her long elegant fingers tapping a rhythm on her thigh. The fingers ceased tapping.

'Hmm... well, I guess you had best deliver it. She would not thank me for holding you up.

'However, as the library is but a few paces away, you hardly need so many escorts. You two, the kitchen is short staffed this evening, you would be better employed helping with supper. Come with me.'

The tone of her voice brooked no argument, so Alain and Stanislaus meekly followed the imperious Abbess of Romsey. John raised his head in time to catch sight of the two boys disappearing down the passageway they had exited from moments before. Alain threw a stricken glance over his shoulder, while Stanislaus demonstrated his feelings on the matter by sticking out his tongue and mimicking being sick.

'What do we do now?' he asked.

Barabal rose, smoothed down the fabric of her dress and tidied her hair. Satisfied with her appearance, she continued on her way.

'We do what we came to do, and worry about the boys later.'

Before following, John had a quick peek round the room. On the walls hung tapestries rich with colour, depicting scenes from the bible. The surrounding alcoves contained panels of religious paintings even John could tell were valuable. A recess in the centre of the wall opposite the doorway, contained a huge cross those entering the convent would not fail to miss. John wondered if they positioned the artefacts to remind people of the house's religious nature, or to display its wealth. Realising he stood doing just what Barabal had told him not to, he sped after her.

The girl waited for him outside an open door, foot tapping impatiently. He glanced into a room with windows running down one side, filtering the last of the day's light. Bound leather books lined the walls. Sitting at a table by the windows was a diminutive woman, head bent, reading.

Her black hair was plaited away from her face to hang down the back of her sober grey gown. Neither handsome nor plain, John would not have looked twice at her. That was until the disturbance in the doorway caused her to look up. Like her future husband's, her violet blue eyes were intelligent and striking.

'Stay here and make sure we are not interrupted,' Barabal commanded, before walking into the room alone.

Stopping in front of the woman she bobbed a curtsy, and waited to be acknowledged. The woman marked her place in the book with her finger before nodding for her guest to speak. Barabal pulled some parchment from her pocket and handed it to the lady.

'Child, you know animals are not allowed inside after vespers, and the bell is almost upon us. Best you take the lamb outside before the reverend mother catches you.'

So engrossed in the scene in the library in front of him, John had not heard the elderly nun come from behind. He literally jumped at the sound of her voice.

'Umm.'

Undecided what to do, John's head pivoted from the nun to Barabal, and back again. To his dismay, the girl was so intent on her conversation with Princess Edith she was completely unaware of anything else happening around her. There would be no help coming from that direction, John was on his own.

'Away with you now,' the nun instructed, her tone giving him no choice in the matter. Leading the lamb out the same way they had entered, John told his guardian, *I knew this would happen. You should have waited out by the cart.*

You had no way of knowing this would happen at all. Stop being so grumpy. There is nothing more you can do here. Barabal has delivered the note, you would not be able to influence the princess' response.

Resisting the urge to stomp his annoyance, he headed for the door, followed by the nun who was intent on ensuring he did as instructed. As he opened the external door, a bell sounded.

'Just put the lamb outside, it will find its way back to the others. We do not want to be late to vespers, do we?'

'Umm, no, I guess not.'

John attempted to make his voice sound as female and breathless as he could, but the nun still glanced quizzically at him. Dropping to the floor to assist Lala outside, he hid from her scrutiny.

Wait by the door, I will come back for you.

With no reply from Lala, John was unsure whether or not the lamb would be there when he returned.

Unable to delay any longer, he stood, closed the door, and followed the woman back into the abbey. The elderly nun led him to an ornate chapel. He silently slipped into a pew beside her, behind rows filled with identical black heads. Someone turned as he sat. A glimpse of the face was enough to tell him Stanislaus and Alain attended evensong as well.

As he waited, the abbess walked from the back to the front of the Chapel. She blessed the nuns before thanking the Lord for the bounty of their day. The service was much like the one he had snuck into with his friend when he wanted to see how a Catholic Church differed from the Baptist one his mother made him attend. His mother had tanned his hide after, for consorting with the devil. How much more annoyed would she be now, knowing he participated in a full Catholic service?

SWAGMAN

A nudge from the nun beside brought him back to the present. Everyone was singing. In his church, songbooks were handed out to everyone as they entered. Here, it appeared the nuns were singing from memory. A frown from the woman told him not joining in was not an option.

Listening to the tune he realised he might cobble something together. He hummed while moving his mouth. The frown of displeasure left her face and she returned her attention to the service.

An age later vespers concluded, and the nuns filed out. His bottom numb from the prolonged sitting, his knees sore from all the kneeling, John creaked upright and followed the others out of the chapel.

Swept along with the crowd, he found himself in a room filled with long tables. Helpers distributed steaming baskets of warm bread and mugs filled with some sort of liquid.

When the others sat, he did as they did. They passed bread and he broke off a chunk, passing the basket on to the girl beside him. He drank what tasted like watered down beer while a nun read passages from the bible. No one spoke. When the reading finished everyone rose and left the dining room to go their separate ways.

Now free of his disapproving shadow, he searched for Alain and Stanislaus. He spotted them clearing tables under the watchful eye of the mother superior. No words were needed to communicate her displeasure at her charge's performance.

Sure that if he waited for them someone would decide he needed something to do to occupy his idle hands, he left the refectory. Striding purposefully to discourage

anyone from stopping him, he soon reached the external door. Glancing around, he made sure no one was watching, then let himself out of the nunnery.

Lala's woolly white coat shone like a beacon in the half-dark. Nestled under a tree, the lamb was curled up, sleeping. Deciding it would be a good idea to try and find Barabal, John was saved the effort by a jerk on his arm. He rounded to be confronted by the angry face of his new friend.

'What were you thinking, just leaving me like that?' She spat at him.

This appeared to be one of those statements Barabal presented as a question, as she did not give him a chance to answer before continuing her tirade.

'As if it were not bad enough those other goons being taken to the kitchen, you deserted me too. Honestly, I should have come alone, regardless of the danger a girl travelling by herself faces.'

Barabal paused to take a breath, and John took the opportunity to defend himself.

'Calm down, will you? While you met with the princess, a nun came along and instructed me to take Lala outside. She gave me no choice. As I released him, the vespers bell rang. I could not very well keep my cover if I missed evening prayers. After, everyone went to supper, so I went along too. There was no chance to slip away without anyone noticing until now.

SWAGMAN

'I found Alain and Stanislaus clearing down tables in the refectory. No doubt they will be along soon as well.'

'Hurmph.' Barabal folded her arms and glared at him, annoyed she was unable to continue letting off steam after such a reasonable explanation.

'You know the gates are locked at vespers.'

Having finished her rant, she voiced the real reason for her worry. As she spoke and he realised the impact of her words, John thought through their options.

'No, I did not know the gates were locked. Perhaps if you would wait here with Lala for the others, I will circle the walls to see if there is anywhere easy enough for us to climb over. It would be best if we left without having to disturb the good sisters.'

Barabal's only response was to sink to the ground beside Lala and lean back against the thick tree trunk, arms tightly clasped around her legs. John felt the need to do or say something to cheer her up, to try and remove the forlorn look from her face.

'Did your meeting with Princess Edith go well?'

Apparently it was the wrong question. Barabal dropped her forehead to her knees and did not answer. After a moment, she looked up, her face a picture of consternation.

'I am not sure. The lady read Prince Henry's letter; sometimes frowning, sometimes smiling. After she finished, she gazed out the window for a long time. When she picked up her pen, she did not appear to know what to write. She restarted a couple of times, but once she got going, she wrote for ages. After a while, she stopped writing and sealed her letter with wax, before handing it to me. She bid me keep it safe and give it only to the prince himself.

'She gave me no idea of the contents, except to say people's lives would be in danger should it fall into the wrong hands.' Barabal sighed and dropped her head back to its former resting place.

'So we have no idea whether or not we have a new queen,' John said, feeling a little frustrated himself. He could not bear to see Barabal so deflated, so he added, 'Well, we did our best. Now all we can do is join Prince Henry as soon as possible.' A tentative smile rewarded his efforts.

With Barabal deflated and in no mood to lead, he decided it was up to him to find a way out. Walking around the back of the abbey, towards what he thought was an orchard and farm, he hoped to find an older section of the wall with a few broken bricks that would allow them to climb over. Or perhaps even a gap they might be able to slip through.

Sometime later, without having found what he was looking for, he debated whether it was quicker to turn back, or continue until he had circumnavigated the grounds. Then a thought hit him. Back tracking a few paces, he found what had sparked his curiosity—an old, gnarly tree with thick branches creating a perfect climbing frame.

It might be the answer to their prayers. Testing his theory, he ascended and leaned over the wall to survey the ground on the other side. A grassy bank grew partway up the old bricks, lessening the distance to the ground to around seven feet. If they held on to the top, lowered themselves down as far as possible, then dropped, they should be able to get over without injury.

Jauntily returning to Lala and Barabal, he found the

girl pacing back and forth. When he asked her what was wrong, she replied Alain and Stanislaus had not yet returned. Gnawing agitatedly on her lip, she would not calm down no matter what John said.

Fretting about lost time, and worrying about how they would be able to catch up with the prince's party after such long delays, John did not help at all when he pointed out the darkness meant it would be too risky for them to begin their journey tonight anyway.

Ignoring his words, Barabal headed over to go and search for the missing boys when a small gap opened and two figures slipped out before shutting the door with a quiet snick behind them.

'Where have you…' Barabal stopped speaking when Alain placed a finger over his lips. He lent forward and pressed his ear to the door. Standing there for some time, the boy eventually straightened up and smiled.

'We finally lost her,' he announced jubilantly, and Stanislaus grinned in relief.

'I was sure we would be scrubbing floors on our hands and knees all night. We cannot help it if we are clumsy. If she had not stood over us watching every move, we would not have been so nervous,' Stanislaus complained.

'We were lucky to get away,' Alain told Barabal. 'The abbess really did not like us. We did not please her on kitchen duty, so she had us scrub pots and pans after dinner until they shone. When he put the pots away, Stanislaus knocked over a pail of milk, and we had to clean that up. We were fortunate someone called her away before we had finished, because scrubbing the rectory floor had been mentioned.'

'She spoke to you after vespers?' Barabal's amazement at such a flagrant disregard for the rules rang clear.

'Well, no,' Alain admitted. 'But she managed to communicate how unhappy she was with us perfectly well without using a single word.'

'Now we are all here, can we at least leave the grounds, have some decent food and a good night's sleep?' Stanislaus asked. 'Bread and small ale is not enough to keep a growing boy fed through the night.'

'Well, at least you have had something to eat. I sat here waiting for you for an age without any food at all.'

Before anyone else started another grumble, John told them his good news, 'I know how we can leave without waking the nun on duty at the gate. Come with me.'

Much to his surprise, they all followed him round to the exit he had found earlier.

'We climb up and drop over the other side. Of course, we will need to hang by our hands from the wall, or else the ground is too far away and we might hurt ourselves.'

The two boys surveyed the tree, then nodded their agreement to his plan.

'I will go last,' Barabal qualified her consent. 'I do not want any of you boys using this as a chance to look up my skirts.'

'I understand your concern, but I am not sure that is going to work,' John told her, earning a steely glare from the girl before he clarified. 'It is quite a long way down the other side and you might need help to get there.'

'You are only saying that because I am a girl,' she stubbornly insisted, hands planted on hips.

'I am saying that because you are by far the shortest

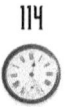

of us all.'

'I am more than capable...' she started to say before John blocked her words out.

She really has a thing about boys looking up her skirts, he complained to Lala.

I do not think you understand. Her underwear does not, umm, how to put this... Women's underwear in this time does not cover private parts.

Oh? Oh!

Appreciating the enormity of the problem, John had an idea. Cutting Barabal off mid-sentence, he said, 'I can climb up and help everyone over the wall. Barabal you can go last and no one will be standing below you on this side. I will lower you down as far as I am able...'

'... and you boys can all turn your backs when I climb down the other side. I am sure I will be able to manage without any further assistance.'

With no objections to his plan, John took off his habit and wrapped Lala inside, making a type of sling over his back. He climbed up the trunk, and straddled the wall.

Stanislaus climbed up next. The boy deftly swung himself over, grasped the top with his hands as he hung his body down. John glanced down and realised the wall was higher than he originally estimated. Before he could stop the other boy, he had let go and fallen to the ground. Rolling, Stanislaus regained his feet with a grin on his face.

'Piece of cake.'

'Right.' John glanced down and saw Alain climbing to meet him. The shorter boy looked over the wall and doubt crossed his face, but only for a moment.

John told him, 'I can hold your hands and lower you

closer to the ground if you like.'

Moving himself into position so his stomach rested on the wall, Alain lowered his body. John grabbed his hands, lowering him an extra arms length. Grunting, as the slight boy was heavier than he looked, his grip was already slipping when Alain let go. He fell to the ground, collapsing in a heap.

Stanislaus rushed over to the boy and helped him up. After checking out all his limbs, Alain grinned back up at John.

'All good.'

'My turn now.' John twisted to see Barabal on the tree beside him.

'It is a long way down,' John warned her. 'You might want Stanislaus to catch your legs at the bottom. I am sure he will respect your... umm... privacy.'

The girl's eyes widened in alarm. 'I am not letting either of those boys stand under me. You can drop me like you did Alain. You there, turn away while I climb down.'

John watched as the boys folded their arms and turned until their backs faced the wall.

'Right,' Barabal said as she eased herself over. John grabbed hold of her hands and lowered her as far down as his arms would let him.

'Barabal, there is still quite a way to go to the bottom, are you sure...' Before he could finish, the diminutive girl let go of his hands and dropped herself to the ground.

'Aww.' Barabal's voice echoed in the evening air as she hit the bank feet first with an audible thud, and collapsed onto the bank. Alain and Stanislaus rushed over.

'It is my ankle,' she told them. 'It twisted as I landed.'

SWAGMAN

Alain was all business. 'Stanislaus, you go help John while I make sure it is not broken.'

The squire moved to stand by the wall. John lowered Lala still in his sling, and the other boy caught him. Then John launched himself over the wall, dropping to the ground without incident. By the time he landed, Stanislaus had freed Lala and was stripping off his own disguise. Bundling his and John's habits together, he stowed them in the nearby bushes, before joining John to check on Barabal.

'Just a sprain,' Alain informed them. 'She will need help back to the cart, but she should be able to walk on it tomorrow.'

John helped Barabal up while Alain went and put his habit with the others. When he returned, he replaced John as Barabal's crutch. As he was closer to her in height, it was more comfortable for her to have his help walking around to the waiting cart.

As they moved past the gate and rounded the wall, a movement caught John's eye. Stanislaus must have seen something too, because he held up his hand to stop them from proceeding any further.

'There are men in the bushes,' he spoke out of the side of his mouth.

'Can we run for it?' John asked, before mentally kicking himself. Of course they could not, not with Barabal's ankle. Besides, the horses were not attached to the cart, so they would not get very far.

The decision was made for them as they were surrounded by armed men.

CHAPTER TEN
PRISONERS

'Who have we here then?' A large man dressed in full chain mail sauntered over to them, hand ready on his sword should they try anything. His florid face sported an oily grin that went well with curly black hair that looked like it had not been washed any time recently.

'Just as we suspected—Mistress Barabal and young Master Stanislaus.'

Do not say anything.

How did Lala guess he had been about to object to Alain and him being ignored by their captor?

To William de Breteuil, and others of his class, if your family do not own land, you are beneath notice. Now please, hold your tongue and let Barabal deal with this.

That is William de Breteuil? He is not at all how Walter Tirel described him. He does not look like a fool, or anyone's pawn.

Tirel may be a little biased. De Breteuil is definitely no one's fool. What he is, is someone who holds true to his beliefs, so be very careful how you behave around him.

John slipped back behind Stanislaus to a position where he could watch proceedings, but hopefully go unnoticed. Barabal shrugged off Alain's supporting arm and stood tall, confronting Prince Henry's enemy. She would not be cowered by anyone.

'How dare you accost us like this. Let us pass and we will be on our way.'

His friend's courage was admirable. As her protector, Stanislaus attempted to make his way to Barabal's side, but the man next to him drew his sword and pointed it at the boy's breast.

'I am afraid I cannot do that until you tell me what you are doing here.' De Breteuil carried on as if unaware of the squire's discomfort.

Frozen in place, Stanislaus glared at the older man, as Barabal drew herself up as tall as her small stature would allow, and haughtily contemplated the noble in front of her.

'Sir, you are not in Normandie now. You have no right to question me here.'

'Know your place, woman, I will not be challenged by the likes of you,' de Breteuil sneered. 'I am an agent of the lawful King of Briton, Robert Curthose, and I will question whomever I choose in his name.'

The men behind them chuckled at Barabal's assertion of her rights being so easily dismissed by the arrogant man. John clenched his fists, wanting to punch them all for being so rude to her but, remembering his night in the dungeon, he held his temper in check.

Stanislaus, however, felt no such restraint. He knocked the sword aside and stood between de Breteuil and Barabal. Nearly as tall as the noble, he was not such an easy target.

'Sir William, as you and I both know, no king is yet crowned, so no one can claim to act on his behalf. Now, Mistress Barabal came to visit a friend, and our master bid me accompany her to protect her from attack. I suggest if you are unhappy with our actions, you should take it up with Robert de Beaumont. Regardless, I am sure he will want words with you about your treatment of those under his protection when we all get back.'

To give Stanislaus credit, he boldly stood eye to eye with the sword wielding lord, showing not an ounce of fear.

'I am unsure whether to be impressed at his gumption, or scared for his foolhardiness.' Alain's whispered comments echoed his own thoughts.

'Why climb over the fence if this was a simple visit to a friend?'

'Why, because these foolish boys got bored waiting for me and took it upon themselves to sneak into the abbey to look around. Not knowing the nunnery's routine, they did not realise the gate closed at vespers. Once inside, they found themselves unable to get out without letting the abbess know of their transgression.' Barabal attempted to lighten the moment.

'I would be inclined to take this on face value, except I am aware Princess Edith resides within these walls. If she aligns herself with Prince Henry, he would have

SWAGMAN

Anglo-Saxon support and there would be no stopping him from stealing the crown. If that happens, Norman influence in these lands would be severely reduced, and I can see no good coming from that.'

William Breteuil stroked his beard thoughtfully.

'Stanislaus, I am surprised to see you helping Prince Henry's cause. I know your master is a staunch supporter of his, but your father would no doubt be in support of his duke, Robert Curthose, being crowned king here in Briton. As a Norman, I am sure he would be in favour of consolidating our power base in Briton.'

Before Stanislaus could answer for himself, Barabal stepped forward.

'Please sire, Stanislaus is just here protecting me. He knows nothing of politics and intrigue.'

'Barabal,' Stanislaus stuttered. 'What are you doing?'

John made to move forward to join Stanislaus in protecting their friend.

Wait. Trust her. I am sure she has a plan.

'Ah, that makes sense. I was sure you would be no lover of the Britons.'

William Breteuil resumed stroking his beard as Stanislaus carried out a short, frantic conversation with Barabal. They spoke so quietly John could not make out a word they said.

Shaking his head, an obstinate expression on his face, the boy blurted out, 'No, my duty is to protect you, no matter what.'

'Enough.' De Breteuil had made up his mind and took control of the situation. 'Tie the others up. Stanislaus, come with me.'

'Why bother with restraining them? We can slit their throats and leave them here. Much less trouble.'

Their captor turned a stare on the man so cold it would turn water to ice. 'Have you no honour? I do not kill helpless children and servants. Do as I bid.'

Turning away in disgust, he took Stanislaus by the arm and dragged him off. The guard nearest to John grabbed hold and led him around the corner towards where they left their cart hours earlier. Alain and Barabal were pulled along behind, with Barabal biting back a yelp of pain as her ankle took her full weight. By the time they reached their captors' camp, her face was ash grey and covered in beads of sweat.

A fire treated them to the smell of a rich stew tended by one of the band's members, who had remained behind to feed his comrades. The aroma wafting from the pot reminded John he was still hungry. Unfortunately, no one offered anything to eat before binding them to one of the cart wheels, and John's stomach grumbled its complaint. Attempting to take his thoughts off food, his mind came upon another problem.

'What happens if I need to relieve myself?'

'Best hope you do not need to,' Alain said.

'What do we do now?' John said as Lala curled up beside him.

'Nothing,' Barabal calmly answered. 'It is all in hand.'

'What?' Alain and John asked in unison.

'Do I need to do all your thinking for you?' Exasperation laced Barabal's words. 'Prince Henry is on his way to London to be crowned king. I told Stanislas to drop this piece of information into his conversation with de Breteuil, who will want to take his men with him to stop that from happening.

'Stanislaus will go with them because de Breteuil now believes he is on Robert Curthose's side. When he comes to say his farewells, I will tell him where I hid the letter from Princess Edith to Prince Henry. He can deliver it.' Barabal sounded smug as she whispered her plan.

'What about us?' Alain asked.

'For all he is supporting the wrong side, William de Breteuil is a godly man. I do not believe he will harm us. He just wants to prevent me from delivering Princess Edith's message. He may leave us to return home on foot, but we can manage that. The important thing is that the letter gets to Prince Henry.'

'I think you are putting a lot of trust in things going the way you worked them out in your head,' John told her.

'And even more trust in Stanislaus not mucking this up,' Alain chimed in.

'I do not see either of you coming up with a better plan.' Barabal turned away from them, well as much as she could within her bonds, showing her annoyance at their lack of praise for her quick thinking.

Lala, is there anything you can do here?

'Who is Lala?' Alain spoke in a low voice.

'You can hear me?' John's head swung round in surprise.

'Of course. All those with magic can hear mind speak if the speaker has not learnt how to, or does not care to, hide their voice.' Alain spoke as though this was something everyone knew.

Lala?

Sorry, I was distracted and let the shield drop for a moment. I guess there is no point putting it back up again now.

'Who is that talking? Are they near? Can they help us?'

'Umm, it is my mentor, and I guess you could say he is near. I was trying to find out if he could help.'

There is nothing I can do. In this form I am extremely limited.

This form? Alain asked

John nodded down at the lamb leaning against his leg and Alain's eyes widened in disbelief.

You call a Great One Lala?

You know he is a Great One?

Of course I do. We spent some time together during your little break in the dungeon. Master Gavin told me he was a Great One and we needed to take care of him. They spent some time talking together. I did not know I could talk with him as well.

Oh. All right. John half shrugged. *Anyway, he told me to call him Lala, so I have no idea what else to call him.*

Well, I guess it must be all right then. If he cannot help, I reckon it is up to me to get us out of this.

Alain leaned back against the wagon, eyes closed. Wondering how taking a nap would help them, John allowed his gaze to roam around the campsite looking for anything to assist their escape.

'What are you two whispering about?' While they were talking, Barabal had shuffled around so she was again able to see them.

John was prevented from answering as de Breteuil appeared by the fire.

SWAGMAN

'Right, you, you and you,' he pointed to three men. 'You are to stay here and guard the prisoners. Keep them here tomorrow and over-night again. The day after tomorrow set them free and let them walk home. That should prevent them getting the message to Henry Beauclerc, and buy us some time.

'The rest, come with me. You too, Stanislaus.'

'See,' Barabal crowed. 'I knew my plan would work.'

Stanislaus moved to say good bye to his friends, but de Breteuil stood in his way.

'Your friend will be cared for, and the servants will ensure she arrives home safely. You can ride one of your cart horses, I assume you can ride without a saddle?'

Stanislaus nodded and reluctantly allowed himself to be led over to choose the best animal from the two that had drawn their cart. De Breteuil paused by the fire on the way back.

'If anything untoward happens to your prisoners I will be most displeased. In fact, if they are harmed in any way, the same shall also be done to you. Understand?'

The men nodded, although one of them mumbled something under his breath as de Breteuil turned away, and the others sniggered their response.

As he prepared his mount, Stanislaus searched for opportunities to come and say goodbye, and to get Princess Edith's letter from Barabal. However, Sir William de Breteuil kept a close eye on him, and the boy had to be satisfied with a brief farewell wave as the men took to the road, chasing Prince Henry and his entourage.

'Merde,' Barabal exclaimed as they left.

Lala did not translate for him, but John understood

the word did not mean anything good.

'What are we going to do now?'

Alain, who until then had appeared to be sleeping, slowly opened his eyes.

'I think I have a plan,' he said, turning his body away from the guards and holding up his unbound hands.

'Hurry up and untie us,' Barabal demanded.

Alain shook his head. 'We must be smart about this. Those men are bigger and stronger than we are. And you cannot run far with that ankle. We need to ensure they will not follow and recapture us.'

'So what is your plan?' John's interest was piqued.

Alain outlined his idea and what he wanted them to do to help. John had to admire his scheme's simplicity and deviousness. Barabal was not so happy, but not having a better alternative, she informed them it was worth a try, if only because her bladder was actually full to bursting.

'Guard. *Guard.* Please, I need to use the privy,' she wailed in a whiney tone that was not at all like her.

'Well, you cannot,' the guard closest to them responded, turning back to his meal.

'What, not at all? We are going to be here for another day. Surely you cannot expect us to go where we sit. The odour will get unbearable, not to mention we would risk getting sick. And you were told to look after us.' Barabal used her best wheedling voice, and the guard sighed.

SWAGMAN

'All right, but you can wait until after we eat.'

'I am not sure I can hold on that long.'

'For goodness sake, Pierre, take her now. I do not want my meal ruined by her complaints.'

Sighing again, the guard lumbered to his feet. Now John joined in the ruse.

'If she gets to go, I want to go too.'

'I am not taking you both. Albert, you take the boy. I suppose you want to go as well.' Pierre nudged Alain with his foot.

'No, I am fine for the moment thank you.'

'Can you not take them both?' Albert asked. 'I do not trust Jean-Paul alone with the food. He will have half it gone before we return.'

'As if you would not do the same,' Jean-Paul retorted.

'Both of you come. This one is tied to the wagon, and if either of these two try to escape we will need an extra person for the chase,' Albert directed, taking charge.

He untied Barabal and John, and glanced quickly at Alain's bindings. Thinking ahead, the boy had wrapped the rope back around his wrists so it appeared he was still securely tied. The three men took the two captives round the other side of the wagon to the privacy of the trees.

Following instructions, John stayed in plain sight while he saw to the call of nature. One of the men went into the woods and found a suitable spot for Barabal. The man outside released her into the shelter of the trees, then both men allowed her enough privacy to complete her task. John took as long as possible, complaining to Jean-Paul having someone watch him put him off going.

Unsympathetic, the man told him, 'Go or do not go.

127

Either way it does not bother me.'

Having delayed as much as he could, John turned to be escorted back to the wagon just as Barabal emerged from the trees. They arrived to find Alain exactly where they left him. Re-securing the prisoners to the wheel, the soldiers returned to finish their evening meal.

'Well?' Barabal whispered, and Alain nodded his head. 'So, what do we do now?' she asked.

'We wait.' A self-satisfied smile hovered around Alain's lips.

The three prisoners watched as the soldiers ate their meal and drunk from their water skins, not once thinking to offer anything to their charges, not that they would have taken so much as a mouthful.

'It is not working,' Barabal hissed.

'Just be patient,' Alain responded.

The minutes passed as though they were hours, and then one of the soldiers, Albert, stood unsteadily. 'What was in that water you gave us, Jean-Paul?'

'It was just water. That skin flint de Breteuil took all the good stuff with him. I do feel a little light headed though, almost like we actually drank ale. Maybe the meat in the stew was a little...' Falling backwards before he finished, the guard appeared to be asleep.

'What? What is going on?' Albert turned and looked at the prisoners. 'What did you do to us?' He started to walk towards them, stumbled, righted himself, swayed, and crumpled to the ground.

Looking from one of his comrades to the other, Pierre seemed uncertain about what to do. Before he could take any action, he started to rock, then, in moments, was fast asleep like the others.

'How long before they wake?' John asked as he moved his hands for Alain to untie him.

As he worked on the ropes restraining Barabal, the boy said, 'Because I had to put the sleeping drought in their stew, I have no idea how much each of them took, or how long it will take to get out of their systems. I would guess about an hour, maybe two at the most.'

'Are you sure you did not kill them?' Barabal rubbed her wrists before adding, 'They are not moving.'

'I will check on them while you sort out the horses.'

Alain went over and leaned down to each man in turn, ensuring they were breathing and their hearts still beat strongly in their chests. He added some wood to the fire, and covered each of them with a blanket before returning.

'They will be fine. In about an hour or so they will wake up with a bit of a sore head, nothing I am sure they have not experienced before.'

'Right,' John said, already in organisation mode. 'I have saddled two horses. I will ride one and take Lala with me. Alain, can you ride? Can you take Barabal with you?'

'What do you mean "take Barabal with you"? I'll have you know I have been riding since before I walked. I will ride on my own, thank you.'

The diminutive girl stood, hands on hips, daring either one of them to disagree. Not willing to argue with her in the mood she was in, John turned to examine the horses seeing if he could find her a suitable mount.

'Their horses are warhorses, would you prefer to take the smaller cart-horse?'

Glaring disdainfully at him, Barabal rummaged through

the back of the cart, pulled out some food and tied it in a bundle, then headed over to the guards' remaining horse.

'This one will do. If one of you would saddle it, and give me a leg up, I will be fine.'

She proceeded to feed an apple to the brutish looking animal, and it nuzzled into her like a kitten.

Alain shrugged his shoulders and went over to help her while John pulled out his swag and bag. He sacrificed a set of his spare clothes to fit the lamb in. Slinging the bag over his shoulder, he walked over to his own horse, tying his bedroll behind before mounting.

By the time they were on their way, leading the cart horse behind them, John estimated they had used up around half of their hour head start. Reluctant to move at more than a walk in the moonlight, he prayed the guards had ingested more of Alain's sleeping draught than the boy believed, otherwise it was possible their captors could still catch them up.

CHAPTER ELEVEN
GUILDFORD

As the sun rose, turning the sky a dusky purple, the road they followed gradually became more visible. The three escapees urged the horses to a trot in an attempt to put some distance between themselves and the guards, who might already be on their trail. Not long after sun-up they stopped to allow their mounts to rest, and to eat some of the food Barabal had liberated from the cart.

Soon after, as they neared the turn off to Winchester, they set the cart horse free. They hoped it would make its way home, or at least find someone to take care of it. Now, able to maintain a steady pace, and with their captors not having caught them up, John stopped looking back over his shoulder. The day grew hotter, and as the sun reached its peak, John's stomach began to grumble.

'Are we stopping any time soon? I am beyond hungry,

and I think the horses could do with a rest.'

'Boys are always hungry.' Barabal snorted.

'I am indeed proof of that, but I also really do need to eat,' John told her.

'I guess there is time to stop. I am to meet with Prince Henry in Guildford tonight. We should be able to make it in time, even with a break. These horses can travel almost twice as fast as the cart.'

They found a shady copse of trees near a stream. Tying the horses to tree branches, John removed their saddles and gave them a drink of water. He joined the others as Barabal was distributing the last of their food. They ate watching the horses nibble at the luscious green shoots by their hooves.

Appetite satisfied, John lay back, the soft grass cocooning him, the sun warming his face. Next thing he knew, Alain was shaking him awake. As he forced his eyes open, he realised the sun was no longer high in the sky. They had slept through the best part of the afternoon.

Rising swiftly to his feet, he found Barabal hurriedly packing up their belongings while Alain went to saddle the horses. Beside him, Lala stretched out lazily. John picked him up, shoving the lamb into his pack as he went to help with their mounts.

Aww, must you be so rough?

Stop grouching. We need to hurry. We slept away most of the afternoon.

John found grumbling without using words not nearly as satisfying as speaking them out loud.

Calm down. We are only fifteen miles from Guildford. We can make the town by sundown at a fast trot.

SWAGMAN

Not sure whether or not to trust the lamb, he asked Barabal, 'How close would you say we are to Guildford?'

Looking around, the girl checked her bearings before saying, 'I have visited only twice before, and only once coming from Winchester, but I would say if we keep a reasonable pace we should arrive by sundown.'

'Well, I guess we needed the sleep and the horses are rested, so not all has been lost.'

Rounding on him, Barabal opened her mouth to say something, then halted, as if she suddenly thought better of it. Her shoulders relaxed and she said, 'Yes, you are right. We might even be earlier than if our journey had gone to plan.'

Moments later they set out on their way to Guildford town. When they slowed the horses, giving them much needed rest, Barabal regaled them with tales of the great township. The town was built around a river crossing and was once called Golden Forde. It was named after flowers that grew on the river banks near the crossing. According to her, the only place in the world better than Guildford was the great city of London. John and Alain exchanged glances, not quite believing anywhere could be as fantastic as their travelling companion claimed.

As the sun sunk low in the sky, they wearily approached their destination. Cresting a hill, they finally spotted the settlement below.

John laughed. 'Barabal, are you sure this town is the amazing place you described? Or do we have further to ride?'

'Well, I am pretty sure this is it,' the girl answered thoughtfully. 'Both times I came before was for the annual market fair, and it was much more festive than today.'

'Right,' John said, thinking from where he sat this walled town appeared far less impressive than Winchester.

Before they rode on, Alain held up a hand to stop them.

'We do not know what to expect when we show up, so it would be better to come in from a side road and approach the castle from behind.'

Barabal considered his suggestion, and shook her head.

'What ever happened between Prince Henry and de Breteuil today, both my masters will be here, and I trust them to protect us. Thinking on it, I believe I will feel much safer if everyone knows we have arrived. I do not think de Breteuil will do anything to us in front of witnesses.'

'I am certain that is true for you,' Alain grumbled. 'Much can happen to us common folk in the halls of a strange place, even in front of others.'

'I will speak to Sir Robert de Beaumont, and ask if he will let you two bed down with Stanislaus tonight. That should keep you safe. Right, shall we go?' This was one of her command questions, but John still did not move.

'Have you two forgotten something?' he asked when they turned to see why he was not following.

'No...' Barabal's brow wrinkled at his question. 'At least I cannot think of anything.'

'I think it has slipped your mind only yesterday you broke me out of a dungeon, turning me into a fugitive,' John patiently explained. 'I do not think it is the best idea for me to be anywhere near Prince Henry or his men at this time.'

'Oh, that,' Barabal waved her hand, swotting his concerns away like an irritating fly. 'You look like any number of commoners now, no one of any rank will take a second look at you. And if they do, I will explain how Walter Tirel's rescuers forced you to go along with them, then abandoned you on the road to Romsey. We found you and took you along to the abbey, meaning to turn you in when we caught up with the prince.

'In the end finding you was quite lucky, because we would not have escaped from de Breteuil's men without your assistance. The Prince must forgive your outspokenness given you are the sole reason we were able to bring Princess Edith's letter to him.'

'Inside of you there is a plan for every situation,' Alain said, his tone suggesting approval of Barabal's quick thinking as he gazed at her in wonder.

'When you have so little control over your own life, I find it is important to manage the people around you,' she responded.

John had to admit Barabal did seem to be an expert at manipulating others. Although her proposal might work, he still was not convinced enough to bet his freedom on it.

'It is a big risk, I would rather not find myself in another dungeon because you misjudged things.'

You need to go with them, no matter your misgivings, Lala commanded.

But..., John started.

I cannot tell you any details. All I can tell you I do not see a dungeon in your immediate future. What I do see is failure should Alain and Barabal continue alone.

'John? Did you hear me?' Barabal brought her horse up beside his, and shook him by the arm, worry marring her face. 'Are you having another one of your turns?'

'No, no, I was just thinking. Do I truly look so different no one will recognise me?'

Realising he needed a reason for changing his mind so easily, having been so adamant just seconds ago, this was the best he could come up with.

'I do,' the girl said confidently. 'Well, at a quick glance at least. I will talk to my lord first thing when we arrive, and ask him to intercede on your behalf with the prince.

'Until then, Alain and you can wait in the kitchen. Boys always hang around where there is food, so no one will think twice about your being there. If you are lucky, perhaps they will take pity on the two of you and give you something hot to eat. No doubt you are both starving again.'

Still reluctant, John followed the other two down the hill towards the smokey haze of Guildford. As they arrived at the outskirts of the town, John chuckled. Alain had boasted about Guildford's size but, even by Australian standards, it was a country village.

The riders stood out among the locals going about their business, all of whom travelled on foot. How the trainee apothecary ever thought the three riders would have been able to sneak into town was a joke.

The streets they rode through were little more than mud paths, with the houses lining them built mainly of wood. Even the defensive castle they headed for was constructed mostly of timber. They did pass one ornate stone building, which Alain explained was a cathedral. It appeared the church had more money to spend on its houses than the crown.

The area outside the castle bustled with activity. A makeshift camp had been set up for Prince Henry's guards, and the castle servants rushed round ferrying food and drink, ensuring everyone had everything they needed.

'See, I told you. There is so much going on here no one has time to look at a common boy, let alone try and remember where they might have seen him before,' Barabal said as Alain helped her dismount.

John scowled at her, hating that she was right, but really a little in awe of her ability to read and manage situations.

'Alain, take the horses round to the stables. When you are done there, you and John should go to the kitchens. I shall go and report to de Beaumont and sort everything out, then I will meet you there.'

As Barabal turned to leave, Alain grabbed her arm.

'You may have been here before, but I have not. Which way do we go to find the stables and the kitchens?'

Releasing an exasperated breath, Barabal spoke slowly and clearly, as if she were speaking to a half-wit.

'If I needed to get to the stables, I would follow others leading horses because there is a high likelihood they are looking for somewhere to house their mounts for the night too.

'Then I would find someone delivering food to the guards and follow them back to where they came from, which is likely to be the kitchens.' Instructions delivered, Barabal yanked herself out of Alain's grip and hobbled slowly towards the castle entrance, her ankle still not quite healed.

'I dislike it when she does that,' Alain said, although his face showed admiration as he followed her retreating figure with his eyes.

'What? Tell you something you might have figured out for yourself if only you had thought about it?' John grinned.

'Yes, exactly that. Annoying, isn't it? Come on, we had best get these animals seen to.'

Following another boy around their age leading a horse, they found the stables. It was over-crowded and the harried stable master directed them round the back, to a field.

'You can unsaddle here, leave the tack there, over the fence, and someone will see to it when there is time. You need to take the saddle bags with you. Our storage space is full up. You can leave the lamb here, it will be quite safe.'

No, you most certainly cannot, Lala told him emphatically.

John considered ignoring the lamb and leaving him behind for some peace, then thought better of it. He still did not know his way around in this century, and Lala might be able to help keep him out of trouble.

'Ah, he is only young. It will be best if he comes with me.'

John picked Lala up and settled him in his bag.

'Fine by me. One less thing to worry about. Which lord do these horses belong to?'

John figured as they had to abandon their cart, they might need the mounts to return to Winchester. So he told the man, 'We are with Robert de Beaumont.'

'Right, the saddle and tack will be stowed with his, although I say this looks more like Duke William of

SWAGMAN

Breteuil's marks on the leather.' The well-built man raised a questioning eyebrow.

'Your eye is keen, sir,' Alain was quick to respond. 'We were a last minute addition to de Beaumont's household, and de Breteuil offered to loan us mounts for the journey.'

'Mmm, all right then,' the man said skeptically as he wandered off. He had too many other things to worry about this day than to do more than ask the question about a discrepancy in markings.

Once again back in the courtyard, the two boys searched for someone serving food. When they arrived earlier, a number of people had been distributing bread and stew, now they were unable to find a single one. Alain's stomach rumbled in complaint, and John's responded in kind. They must have looked either quite forlorn, or likely to cause trouble, as they had not been standing around long when a group of guards wandered over to them.

'What are you young 'uns up to? Not causing mischief I hope.'

John was looking at the ground, trying to hide his face in a not-hiding-his-face sort of way, leaving Alain to speak for them both. Keeping his tone friendly and sticking to the truth, the boy answered.

'Our mistress, Barabal, instructed us to meet her at the kitchens after we sorted the horses, but we do not know where they are, and we have no idea where to start looking.'

The man laughed. 'Normally you would follow your noses, but with the great unwashed camping out here in the courtyard you would never find your way.

'Tom, show the boys where they need to go, and do not be hanging around after trying to fill that bottomless pit you call a stomach. We are meant to be on guard duty, so meet us at the west gate when you are done.'

The guard nodded at the youngest of the group, a boy not much older than them. The young guard's expression changed to delight when he heard his new orders, then resignation as his commander's final words forestalled his chance for an extra snack.

'Come on,' he said. 'Kitchen's this way.'

Tom led them around the side of the castle, away from the stables, weaving so expertly between the crowd he had to stop a couple of times for the boys to catch up. Finally they walked through an archway into a courtyard, and on towards the castle's only stone building.

Through the doorway, John made out a cooking fire with a cauldron swinging over it. Even though the staff were busy clearing up, this one sight gave him hope he might still eat a hot meal this day. It had been so long since he had eaten anything warm; his mouth salivated at the thought.

'Kitchen's over there.' Tom pointed, and prepared to leave.

'Ah, before you go, can you tell us if Duke William de Breteuil has arrived, and where his men might be?' John asked.

'Most of the time I am not really interested in the comings and goings of the high and mighty.' The boy paused before continuing, 'but he created such a ruckus when he arrived today. He and his men rode in here not long after the prince, like the very devil was chasing them.

'Prince Henry was busy seeing to his men, but de Breteuil strode up and started haranguing him. Yelling

140

at Prince Henry, he called him a cheat and accused him of killing the king. They almost came to blows, and their guards drew weapons. My master called in his men to keep the peace until they both calmed down.'

The delight on Tom's face as he spoke told them how much he enjoyed telling his story. Seeing this, John decided the talkative boy might be pumped for more information.

'Do you know where de Breteuil is now?'

'Yes, he took over some rooms in one of the towers. He posted a guard outside the door. Says he fears for his life with Prince Henry staying in the same place, but he will be damned if he lets an upstart steal a crown that rightfully belongs to Robert Curthose. He is an odd one. My master would never let anything happen to any of his guests. Are you part of his retinue?' Thinking perhaps he might have over-stepped the mark, Tom looked worried.

'Sounds like he was in a state,' John said. Then quickly added, 'Do not worry, we are not his men.'

'We are castle staff from Winchester, we came here with Mistress Barabal.' Alain reassured the young guard. 'One of our friends travelled here with de Breteuil though, and we had hoped to find him this evening if possible.'

'I can take you to him,' Tom said helpfully. 'That is unless you planned to eat.'

'We want to do both,' Alain told him. 'I thought you might join us for a quick bite, and afterwards take us to find our friend, Stanislaus.'

Tom's expression changed from pleased to worried in a matter of seconds. 'I want to help you, but orders are to go directly back to my duties at the west gate.'

'It is all right, you can tell your captain that Mistress Barabal asked you to stay and help us get around. Believe me when I say your captain will be unlikely to argue with that particular lady, and she will be grateful for your help.' John hoped to persuade the boy to stay.

'If you think it really will be all right, I could really do with a little more to eat. Supper was over an hour ago.'

The guard's face brightened considerably as they entered the kitchen, the smell of food driving away all thoughts of duty. After he helped them wheedle some stew and fresh bread from the cook, the three boys took their meal outside. Finding a bench against the wall, they sat down to eat.

CHAPTER TWELVE
CONSPIRACIES AND CONFRONTATIONS

H aving almost finished their meal of meat stew served in a hollowed out piece of bread, John leaned back and allowed his food to settle. Alain called the bread a trencher, and John marvelled at the useful invention. The bread mopped up the gravy, and you simply ate it when you were done.

Alain also said people fed it to the pigs once they had eaten what was inside, but John did not understand why you would waste such wonderful food. When no one was looking, he fed a little bread soaked in meat juices to Lala, who had curled up by his feet. The lamb immediately spat it back out.

It does not taste the same in this form.

You keep saying this form, does that mean you are not an actual sheep?

Of course not, did you truly think I was? Lala transmitted an impression of amusement along with the words.

Well, to be honest, I had not thought too much about it. On reflection though, I guess it is unlikely you would be. I imagine a Great One would be more like a god, having no body at all.

In fact…

'John, quit wool-gathering. Tom said he would take us to where Stanislaus is staying if we are ready.' Alain shook his arm.

'Oh. All right.'

John stuffed the last of his meal in his mouth and placed Lala securely in his pack. Following Tom across the courtyard, he soon found himself at a wooden tower.

'Is he in the dungeon?' John asked.

'No,' Tom stared at him like he was not quite right in the head.

'Not all castle towers contain dungeons,' Alain explained. 'Some house guards, or provide additional rooms used for guests.'

'Oh.'

John's anxiety disappeared as their guide led them up some winding stairs. Standing on the slightly larger step leading to a doorway, they were stopped by a burly man.

'What do you want?' the man asked gruffly.

'Ah, we just want to see if our friend is inside,' Alain said.

'Well, you cannot. Go away.'

John looked at Alain, who shrugged his shoulders. He too appeared unsure of the protocol in this situation.

SWAGMAN

Before they could think of anything to say to change the guard's mind, Tom stepped between them.

'My lord asked me to accompany these boys and ensure they met with their friend. I am sure you do not want to disrespect his hospitality.'

The guard glared at Tom. Just when John thought they had no option but to leave, he reluctantly stepped aside.

'I guess a couple of minutes will not hurt. Keep the door open though, and no funny business.'

Opening the door for them, he ushered them through and half-closed it behind. Leaving just enough of a gap to make sure they behaved.

They found themselves in a surprisingly large room dominated by a four-poster bed. By the far wall sat a makeshift wooden pallet with a straw mattress and a thick woollen blanket. Stanislaus slept on top, mouth open, snoring.

'It must be so hard being taken captive by a noble man,' Alain whispered.

'Wha... what?'

Stanislaus half-opened his eyes, blinked, and peered blearily across the room at his visitors.

'Hey, Alain and John. You made it.' He swung his legs over the side of the bed, stood and stretched in a single fluid movement.

'When did you arrive? Have you come to take me back to Sir Robert de Beaumont?'

'Take you to de Beaumont? What do you mean?' John asked. 'We thought you sided with de Breteuil and so you are staying with him now.'

Looking to the open door Stanislaus winked. 'I am.

He knows I am on his side over this thing about Prince Henry and the crown. I fully support his notion we Norman's should take back control of you Britons. I mean you had no real culture until we arrived. But he told de Beaumont I am his hostage. I think it is to make sure no one here attacks him.'

'Oh, well I guess you will not be leaving with us then,' John said.

At these words Stanislaus began making some weird movements with his mouth. Lala's translation magic did not appear to be working, because John could not make out what he was trying to say. Looking to Alain, the boy turned both his hands outwards in a "search me" gesture.

Lala, I need a little help here. Can you work out what is going on?

The lamb wriggled a little and his head popped out of the bag. He examined Stanislaus for a bit and snuggled back inside.

Well?

He is mouthing "get me out of here".

'Oh,' Alain said, and John realised Lala had decided not to shield this conversation.

He felt the bag settle as the lamb made himself comfortable again, having completed his task. John hesitated, allowing Alain to take control of the situation.

'Everyone is still eating in the hall, do you want to come down to the kitchens for some supper? You can be back here before de Beaumont sees you out and about without a guard. That way de Breteuil can keep up his little ruse, that is if you are truly not being held prisoner.'

'No, the man outside is for show.' Stanislaus went to

the door. 'Hey, I am just nipping down to the kitchen with these boys for some food. I will be back before dinner in the hall is over, so no one will know I even left.'

The guard planted himself in the doorway, arms folded across his chest, blocking their exit.

'I do not think that is such a good idea.'

'Yes, it is. I am hungry and I would like to eat with my friends.'

The man mountain stood strong, not moving a muscle.

'You are behaving as though I really am a prisoner here...' Stanislaus started only to be interrupted by their new friend Tom, who John had forgotten was in the room.

'And that cannot be, as my lord would need to be informed of what crime has been committed for one man to hold another captive in his house. Should I fetch him over so we can discuss the matter?'

'I think you had all best stay here until Sir William de Breteuil returns.'

'I am unable to do that, I am afraid. I was ordered to escort these boys to find their friend, then report for duty. I am late already. My captain will come looking for me any minute. So, while I would like to stay and enjoy your company, I am afraid I must leave.'

Tom moved, pushing the guard backwards into the corner. The boy then stood in front of him, making it difficult for the man to move.

'Run now,' the young guard instructed.

The others did not need a second invitation, they were out the door and off. As they exited the doorway of the tower they stumbled over a man about to enter, causing him to drop the bottle he held. Alain stopped to help him to his feet, and was distracted by the broken vial on the ground.

'Come on,' John tugged at Alain's arm while checking behind them to see how close their pursuer was.

'Wait a minute.' Alain turned back. 'Are you Master Bernard, the castle apothecary?'

The man paused, dusting himself off and stared at Alain. 'I am. Who wants to know?'

'Oh, pardon me, sir, but I am Alain, apprentice to Master Gavin of Winchester. I just wanted to apologise for causing you to break a precious glass vial. Can I replace it with something from my own stock?'

'Well, ah, thank you for your offer, young sir, but what Duke de Breteuil required is not something you would be carrying round on your travels.'

John noticed Master Bernard's demeanour altered when he realised he spoke to a fellow apothecary.

'Perhaps not the exact same cure, but maybe something else equally able to deal with his problem.' Alain continued to press, trying to find out what the other apothecary had been delivering to Prince Henry's enemy.

'Sorry, but Sir William de Breteuil specifically ordered some Fowler's Tonic, and an especially concentrated dose. It seems with all this travelling around the country he is not feeling as sprightly as he might. I brewed a double batch, and what he is paying will more than cover two deliveries and two glass vials.'

No longer flustered, the elderly man busied himself sweeping the pieces of glass into the grass with the toe of his shoe, away from trampling feet. Meanwhile, John started edging Alain away as sounds from within the tower grew louder.

SWAGMAN

'Oh, well of course I would not bring anything like that with me. It would need to be stored separately, seeing as I would not want anyone to mistakenly take something so dangerous. And it has so few uses, it would just waste space. I am sorry again for causing your fall.'

'All is forgiven, I was a young boy myself once. I remember what it is like having a bit of spare time and a lot of excess energy.'

With the path now clear, the man bustled off, John guessed to go and fill another vial so he could over-charge de Breteuil. While watching Alain as he stared thoughtfully after the older man, John was hit from behind and stumbled before regaining his balance.

'Sorry,' Tom gasped. 'Run!'

The four boys took off just as Stanislaus' guard burst through the tower door. Running as fast as they were able, the boys followed Tom between the tents in the makeshift camp. Eventually they reached the west gate, and Tom skidded to a halt right in front of his captain. By the expression on the man's face, he was none too happy to see his errant charge. Anticipating a lecture, John came to Tom's rescue.

'My Mistress Barabal sends her apologies, sir. She asked Tom to help us out for a bit. He argued strongly he needed to return to his duties, but she is very persuasive. I am sure if you go to the palace early tomorrow, she will thank you for loaning us your Tom.'

The captain glared at John as though he wanted to say something. Expelling a deep sigh, his expression softened and he said, 'Who am I to question what my betters do? They do not care about any extra work they cause for us.' He spun on his heel, and Tom gave them a farewell wave and a grin as he followed.

'Thank goodness, it looks like our guard friend was put off by the presence of the Guildford men,' Stanislaus informed them when they were alone.

He an Alain checked the crowd to make doubly sure, but John stood his ground, sizing up the apprentice apothecary.

'So what was that all about?' John finally asked. 'The man we knocked down, something he said worried you.'

A shadow crossed over Alain's face. 'It might be nothing, but Fowler's Tonic contains arsenic, and a strong dose will contain lots of it. It is not a well known curative, but the Roman's used it a lot. For the most part, it is used to restore energy, but too much can take a person's life. If anyone else ordered it, I would not worry, but...'

'... but it is de Breteuil, and you are worried he might use it on Prince Henry?' John finished and turned to Stanislaus. 'Do you know anything about de Breteuil's plans. Has he spoken of poisoning Prince Henry?'

'Not that I heard. But I am not sure he fully trusts me.'

'We need to find out whether or not he intends to use the tonic for himself,' Alain said. 'Stanislaus, I am afraid you must return to de Breteuil and keep up your pretence as a loyal follower.'

Stanislaus sighed. 'Must I really? He is so boring, always going on about God and doing the right thing, and how we Normans are far superior to anyone else. And his men do not appreciate a joke at all. Also, I think he might be holding me hostage, for real.'

Stanislaus was so downcast John considered telling

him not to return. Fortunately, Alain displayed no such weakness.

'Yes, you must Stanislaus, you are the only one who can find out what he is up to. I am sure he would not hurt you as he would not want de Beaumont, or your father, as an enemy. I would not ask, but you can appreciate how important this is.'

'After running away, he will no longer believe I am on his side,' Stanislaus said hopefully.

'If you hurry, you may still get back before he returns. Tell the guard you just wanted a bit of fun. With any luck he will not want to admit you ever left the room because it might get him in trouble as well,' John told his new friend, not wanting to send the boy back to his prison, but also not seeing any other way to gather the intelligence they needed.

'It will be an act of sacrifice and bravery, and you will be a hero should we save Prince Henry from coming to harm,' Alain told him.

The idea of being the prince's saviour brought a smile to Stanislaus' face.

'Yes, I will be facing grave danger to save our future king. Of course I will be hailed a hero after he is crowned. Best I hurry back before anyone important finds me here. See you later.'

Without further thought, the boy sprinted away, hoping to be safely back in his rooms before the nobles of the land left the dining table.

'I sometimes wish it was not so easy to persuade Stanislaus to do what I want. He is brave, and a skilled fighter with an enormous heart, but he is not one of the world's great thinkers,' Alain said.

'If we thought his life truly in peril we would not ask him to do this.'

John's attempt to raise their spirits after having returned their friend to the lion's den fell a little flat.

If it is any consolation, I do not see anything untoward happening to the boy in the immediate future. In fact, there is a potential promotion for Stanislaus if this all goes well.

Alain's eyes widened as Lala allowed him in on the conversation. 'While that is nice to know, I still feel like a louse,' he said. 'But it is too late now. Come on, let us go and find Barabal. She will be looking for us, and we need to tell her everything we found out.'

It had not taken Barabal long to track down the prince's people. In the crowded dining hall, Prince Henry and his men were easily found as they sat on display at the high table. From the look of things, supper was not long over as half empty dishes still sat untouched. No one moved because their host still plied his high born guests with wine, and while he and the prince enjoyed a drink, everyone else must stay.

Standing in the doorway, she tried to attract her master's attention. Unfortunately Robert de Beaumont was so deep in conversation she was unable to do so. Vexed, because she could not just enter the hall and interrupt him or the prince, Barabal glanced around at the gathered nobles, trying to decide her next move. As her gaze swept the room, another pair of eyes met hers with surprise.

William de Breteuil elbowed his neighbour in the ribs, and they both stared towards Barabal. De Breteuil called for his squire, speaking animatedly to him, he gestured and pointed to the girl. This was not good. She could not let herself be caught before talking with the prince. As she went through her options, a serving girl entered beside her, carrying a pitcher of wine.

'Ah, the prince asked me to bring the next jug to his table,' Barabal said, grabbing the pitcher.

Expecting the girl to let go when addressed by her superior, she was surprised when the servant did not even loosen her grip.

'I know, I heard him giving the order. Now, let go and let me get on with my work.'

Haughtily, Barabal stared at the servant to no effect. At that moment, she realised the rather stunning girl hoped she might catch the prince's attention when she served him. He did have a reputation for enjoying the company of beautiful women, and he was generous to those he took a liking to while they were with him. With that mindset, she no doubt believed Barabal had the same interest in the prince and wanted to do away with the competition.

'Well, Prince Henry requested another pitcher a moment ago for my master, Robert de Beaumont,' Barabal improvised. 'I am to take this one to him, perhaps you could help me out and fetch another to take to the prince?'

Hoping the girl would be happy enough now she would be serving Prince Henry, Barabal glanced over the taller girl's shoulder to find William de Breteuil's squire close by. While the servant pondered her proposal, Barabal took a chance and grabbed the jug away from her.

'Thank you ever so much,' she told the stunned maid. Carefully carrying the wine so it did not spill, she walked up the middle of the room, certain the squire would not accost her in front of so many people.

She was wrong. The boy dodged the serving girl and followed closely behind. He grabbed her arm, halting her progress and sloshing wine on to the rush strewn floor. Luck was on her side though, as de Beaumont glanced up to identify the cause of the commotion, and frowned as he spotted Barabal being accosted.

'What is the meaning of this?' He stood as he questioned the pair.

'The wine you asked for, sir?'

Barabal hoped de Beaumont would understand her cryptic comment and come to her rescue. Her lord's expression changed from confused to angry as he realised his charge had been assaulted by the young man gripping her arm.

'About time too, mistress. You there, what are you doing man-handling my wife's companion like that?'

Placed in the spotlight by someone of superior rank, the boy let Barabal go and took a step backwards.

'Bring the wine up here, girl, and, you, return to your duties.' Sir Robert de Beaumont sat back down, expecting them to carry out his orders without further incident.

The squire sent a questioning glance to de Breteuil, who glared back. His annoyance at being thwarted written all over his face. Shaking his head in disgust, the baron beckoned the boy back over.

With her stomach still churning, Barabal walked with apparent calm up to the top table and started pouring wine. De Beaumont ignored her as he would any other person serving at the table. Only the fact he watched Sir William de Breteuil over the rim of his goblet as he sipped his wine gave any indication this incident was more than it appeared on the surface.

As she served, she noticed one of the other guests leaned in and spoke to de Breteuil. Robert de Beaumont took the opportunity to speak to her while the man was distracted.

'Stay behind my chair with Squire James. I cannot leave while the prince remains, so we need to wait until after the meal for you to explain to me what is going on, and why de Breteuil's man attacked you in public.'

Trying hard not to let her emotions show, Barabal placed the wine pitcher down and took her place beside James. As she waited, she worried. Now the baron knew they had escaped his clutches, de Breteuil would send someone to find Alain and John, and she had no way of warning them.

Throughout the rest of the evening meal, she checked to make sure de Breteuil's squire remained behind his master's chair, awaiting instructions. A couple of times when she looked, Barabal found the lad staring angrily back at her, and she quickly turned away. Sure that while he remained the other boys were safe, she relaxed a little.

The head table continued to drink and talk, enjoying the evening. Although people were beginning to fuss and fidget, no one could leave until Prince Henry did. It did not help her temper any that her stomach was loudly protesting its lack of food by the time the prince stood, signalling the end of the meal. She did not know how the waiting staff managed to do this every night.

Stifling her sigh of relief, Barabal followed Sir Robert de Beaumont out of the hall and through the door into one of the castle's common rooms. As she passed the serving girl from her earlier altercation, she received a knock that almost toppled her off her feet. The maid was not pleased at having been bested.

While they waited for Prince Henry to deal with some other matters, Barabal took time to recount the details of their journey to her master. She left out the part where they rescued John before leaving. However, she did mention how they found him by the road on the way to Romsey and had brought him along with them. De Beaumont agreed he would talk to the Prince about allowing John to remain free in light of his help.

They continued their wait in silence as Prince Henry concluded his business with the other nobles. As they waited, Barabal's stomach rumbled and she coloured in embarrassment. Sir Robert asked James to fetch her some food.

A few minutes later she was seated in the corner with the squire, eating some bread and cheese. When the boy stole food off her plate, she pretended not to notice as he would not have a chance to eat until his master dismissed him.

Once finished, she drowsily closed her eyes, only to be awakened by a sharp kick to the ankle. Glaring at James with her most withering look, she realised the room had emptied and the prince and Sir Robert de Beaumont watched her, waiting for her to answer their question.

'Sorry, I must have dozed off. Can you please repeat the question, sire?'

'I hear you had quite a journey today.' Prince Henry smiled. 'I am not surprised you are exhausted. I asked if Princess Edith sent an answer with you?'

'Oh, yes, of course, sire.'

Barabal stood, reached into her pocket and handed him the letter.

'And William de Breteuil did not read this?' Henry queried her before opening it.

'No, sire, it did not seem to cross his mind to search me for a letter. From his words, I understood he believed I had a verbal message from Princess Edith, and by detaining me the message would not reach you.'

Henry laughed out loud, 'It probably never occurred to him a woman of your station, and an Anglo-Saxon to boot, was capable of reading or writing.'

Turning away from the others for privacy, Prince Henry broke the letter's seal and began to read. When he turned back, the smile on his face told Barabal whatever the princess said was to his liking.

Moving impatiently from one foot to the other, Barabal hoped the Prince would dismiss her soon. She wanted to find out if John and Alain were all right, but first she needed to find a privy.

Deciding Barabal must still be in the castle, John and Alain joined the servants cleaning up after the evening meal. They had just dropped a load of dishes back in the kitchens and were returning to the great hall when they came face to face with William de Breteuil. Turning to run, they found their way blocked by two of the lord's guards.

'Mistress Barabal's servants. I am surprised to see you here. You evidently have hidden talents.'

'Well hidden.' One of the guards snorted and earned a withering glare from de Breteuil.

'Your mistress managed to make contact with the prince, in fact she is in with him now.' De Breteuil nodded towards the door at the back of the hall.

'Then you lost.' John finally found his voice, though his gut still churned with fear.

'The game is not over until Prince Henry wears the crown on his head, boy. This is a minor setback. There are other ways to stop the coronation.'

'Then why bother with us?' Alain had also found his voice, although it wavered a little.

'So you can pass a warning on to that little upstart Barabal. Stay out of the dealings of your betters, and stay out of my way. If you do not, I will be forced to start thinking of ways to sideline you... permanently.'

Poor Stanislaus, what had they let him head back into? John turned to Alain, who glared at de Breteuil.

'We Britons want nothing of your Norman Duke. If Prince Henry is made king, Saxon blood will run through the veins of the next King of Briton. That is something worth fighting for.'

John wondered where Alain suddenly got his courage

from, but he had to admire the boy for standing up to the bullying noble.

'Bah, you Saxons were nothing until our great Duke William conquered you and became your first King William. We brought culture and discipline to this uncivilised part of the world. Without Duke Robert Curthose being crowned your next king, you will fall back into savagery and your civilisation will fall.'

De Breteuil stood taller, towering over Alain, who looked smaller in the larger man's shadow. The boy was undaunted, in spite of the physical intimidation.

'Robert Curthose cannot administer the lands he holds now, something you and the other barons are relying on. We will be a nation without a head, free to be pillaged by you and your Norman brethren. I think it is more likely Briton will fall apart under his rule than Prince Henry's, and there are many of us prepared to fight to prevent that from happening.'

Alain himself stood taller as he spat the words at the despised Norman baron.

'Bah, I do not have time to bandy words with a common boy. Pass on my warning to Barabal and the man she serves, Prince Henry's lackey. Come.'

The nobleman departed and, as suddenly as they had been accosted, John and Alain found themselves alone. Relief surged through his body as John leaned against the wall. Finally he stopped trembling and found his voice.

'Wow, Alain, I did not realise you felt so strongly about what we are doing. I thought it was just a bit of an adventure for you.'

Alain, who had not moved a muscle since they first encountered William de Breteuil, turned and stared at John in disbelief.

'You must be joking. I risked everything to break you out of the dungeon, just because a Great One said without you Prince Henry would not be crowned king.

'Do you have any idea what it was like living under the Williams? My father lost his lands when William the Conqueror handed them over to one of his men, simply because my father supported his sworn lord against the Norman invasion.

'Then his son, William Rufus, ruined this country when he took the crown because he wanted to follow in his father's footsteps. Intent on expanding his holdings, he thought he could take the Welsh on and win. He lost time and time again. All those resources and men wasted simply so he could extend his power, while the people of Briton starved. Bring civilisation, huh? They stripped the country of everything good and tried to wipe out our Anglo-Saxon identity.

'While he is of Norman heritage, at least Prince Henry is offering to return some power to the people of Briton, and he will marry a Saxon wife. I would give my life for that. Barabal feels the same.'

'Oh.'

It was hardly an adequate response in the face of Alain's passion, but he was unable to think of anything else to say.

'Why are you doing this then? You are not from here, what have you to gain by helping us?' John opened his mouth to reply, but Alain continued speaking. 'Master

SWAGMAN

Gavin assures me the lamb who talks to our minds is a Great One, one of the Time Guardians. Are you one of them too?'

John frantically tried to think of some believable story to tell, but stopped himself. Alain had been brutally honest with him, perhaps he deserved the same honesty in return, even if he was unlikely to believe it.

'Yes, Lala is a Time Guardian. I am not though. He transported me from a time in the future to ensure Henry takes up the crown and the Charter of Liberties is enacted. If your court system is not changed, the problems we face in my time will be far worse than they are now. So, I guess you could say I came here to fight for the future of my country and my people.

'Lately though, I believe Lala also might have brought me here so I could learn another way to bring about change where I come from.'

John expected Alain to at least laugh at him, or to call him mad, but the other boy tipped his head to the side as he thought, then shrugged.

'That means we both have something to lose if Prince Henry does not become king. Come on, we still need to find Barabal.'

'What about Stanislaus? I feel very uneasy after that run in with de Breteuil. Should we not at least try and rescue him from the man's clutches?'

Now Alain laughed. 'That would be worse for him than leaving him there. William de Breteuil would know Stanislaus is only pretending to support the Norman cause rather than just suspecting it, and we would still be no closer to finding out what he has planned.

'Now, the one thing you can say for Stan is he has a knack for saving his own skin. He will be over convincing de Breteuil he is his new best friend. Stan may be an open book, and he may be readily talked into doing things he perhaps should not, but he is also cunning. And he has the gift to be able to talk his way into getting the best out of any situation.'

If Alain was not worried, John was not going to argue. After all, he had known the young squire longer.

At that moment, the door at the end of the room opened and a weary Barabal emerged. Her face brightened when she saw her friends. Prince Henry followed her out, and John's stomach lurched for a second time that evening.

'There you are. I thought I was going to have to hunt through every building and all the grounds for you both when James said he could not find you in the kitchens.'

Barabal had the ability to tell you off while making you feel pleased to see her at the same time.

'Our escaped prisoner has returned,' Prince Henry said looking at John and Alain. 'Mistress Barabal says I should thank you both for the letter from my future wife making its way to my hands.'

Learning from his last experience, John said nothing, and the prince laughed out loud.

'She is right, young John, you have learnt your place. Is she also correct when she says where you come from all may speak their mind to your leaders, no matter what their rank?'

When John did not answer, Prince Henry told him, 'I give you permission to speak freely in my presence.'

With the prince having given him leave to talk, John's words came tumbling out.

'My apologies for the other night, sire. If I had known more of your customs, I would have kept silent. I only spoke as I did because where I come from a person can disagree with our rulers and not be thrown into prison. That is unless they speak lies or untruths, then they might very well find themselves locked up.'

'What a noisesome place it must be. How can anyone rule if everyone must speak their mind before a decision is made?' Prince Henry rubbed a weary hand across his forehead as he considered what John had told him.

John said nothing. He knew giving away too much about the future could have unforeseen consequences, so he kept quiet.

'Master John, with everyone having their say, decisions must take an age to be made, but no country could be ruled that way. I think perhaps there is more to this system of government than you said. Is there more?' The prince pinned John with a steely gaze, and the boy wriggled uncomfortably.

Before answering he weighed up the consequences of giving Prince Henry more details over what he might do if John refused to answer. With Lala offering no advice, he finally decided he had no choice but to respond to the future monarch.

'It does not quite work like that, sire. In my country every few years we choose people to govern us, and to advise the king. Those people make the laws guiding our society by winning a majority vote. There are paid officials who ensure the rules are followed.'

Henry's eyes grew wider with surprise the more John spoke. When the boy was done, he stroked his beard as he wandered over to the fireplace.

'So, if we did that here, the barons and landholders would elect a council, and the council would decide what happens for all. I have never heard the like, but it might sort of work. Robert, imagine if instead of all the barons coming to court, they elected a few to represent their views. I would not be forced to listen to so many tiresome voices objecting to my every move.'

John held his breath, wondering if he had gone too far, expecting a lecture from Lala at any moment.

Sir Robert de Beaumont laughed before he weighed in on the conversation. 'I do see the appeal, sire, and it would be perfect if you could decide or influence who the barons would choose as their representatives.

'Imagine though, if they selected your most vocal enemies. Those men might perhaps feel justified in opposing you more aggressively if they considered themselves having been raised in status by their peers.'

Prince Henry drew back as though he had been bitten by something nasty. 'You are right, Robert. I do not want any of that bunch to believe they have more influence than another. At least with all the barons here, I can look them in the eye as we make decisions. It is easy enough to identify those I need to bribe or bully to get what I want.'

Well done, Lala told John. *For a moment history stood*

poised to change, and not in a good way. Now everything is back running as it should.

'Well, at least I now understand why you spoke out as you did, John. It is clear that landholders where you come from have more say in government than they do here. I grant you permission to do the same when we are in private, but you must keep to your place when other people are around.'

'Thank you, sire,' John answered, not correcting the prince's assumption he came from a higher station in life, not wanting to risk being returned to the dungeons.

'Now, since we are near to London, I suggest you come along with us. After I am crowned, you can head back to Romsey with Barabal. Princess Edith has requested Mistress Barabal be included in her retinue, and you might as well continue your duties as escort to her for the time being.'

His final command given, Henry retreated to his room and shut the door.

De Beaumont turned to Alain and John. 'Now you two have the look of boys who have been up to something. Tell me all the details.'

'Umm.' John briefly considered not saying anything, but de Beaumont forestalled that idea.

'You may as well tell me everything, no good ever comes from trying to hide things.'

'Oh, no,' Barabal cried. 'What did you boys do while you were out of my sight? Honestly, can I not trust you to keep out of trouble for even a short time?'

'Why do you always assume we caused the trouble?' Alain seemed more annoyed Barabal had jumped to conclusions than being wary of Sir Robert de Beaumont finding out what they had been up to.

'Because you have been running, and I know you did not wait in the kitchens as I asked because James did not see you there when he went to fetch food for me.' She stopped speaking as something dawned on her. 'Did you find Stanislaus? Yes, you did. Why is he not here? Did you lose him again?'

'Can she read our thoughts?' Alain asked John.

'It would appear so.'

Do not be so daft you two, she is an extremely bright girl with an aptitude for reading people.

'Come on, you two, tell me what happened.'

Barabal planted her hands on her hips, and John looked pointedly at Robert de Beaumont then at Alain, willing the boy to hold back key details of their evening until they were alone. De Beaumont intercepted the glance.

'I saw that, young man. I am not going anywhere until I have heard everything. So the sooner you start, the sooner we can all get some sleep before leaving for London at first light.'

The noble gestured to a table and, when they were all seated, he started.

'Well?'

Resigned to the fact they had no choice but to tell their tale, John let Lala out of his bag. The lamb wandered over to the fire and curled up. At first glance, anyone would think he slept, but John knew he kept a close eye on the door, ensuring their privacy. In the meantime, Alain had begun telling their adventures. De Beaumont sat back and regarded them both with a twinkle in his eyes, which changed to dismay when he heard about their run in with William de Breteuil.

'I do not know whether to be impressed at how much you learnt in such a short time, or annoyed at the havoc you caused in a delicate situation. I am leaning towards the latter, not least because you allowed my ward Stanislaus to return to a dangerous situation.'

'What about the fact de Breteuil is likely going to try and poison Prince Henry?' Alain asked. 'Surely that is important enough for Stanislaus to risk himself?'

Shaking his head, Sir Robert de Beaumont displayed his displeasure. 'Alain, all the royal family are aware of how easy it would be for someone to do away with them using poison. That is why any food served to the prince is tasted first.'

Alain remained unconvinced.

'The vial Master Bernard had contained arsenic. A big dose will kill quickly, but smaller doses over time can go undetected, and the prince would appear to become sick with a regular illness. If de Breteuil planned this well enough, we may not realise he was poisoning Prince Henry until it is too late.'

Robert de Beaumont considered this information but Barabal spoke up before he could answer.

'I agree de Breteuil might consider this if he had time. Alain, how long would this type of slow poisoning take?'

'Depending on how much he ingests, it might take weeks, or even months.'

'I think we can rule that out then. De Breteuil does not want Prince Henry to be crowned king, and the ceremony will happen in two days' time. He will need to go for a bold move,' Barabal informed them.

De Beaumont nodded his agreement. 'Barabal is right. He will need to kill Prince Henry as soon as possible, in a way that cannot be traced back to him. Especially so soon after one death in the family already this week.'

As he listened to the conversation something occurred to John.

'Umm, talking of murderers, did you recapture Walter Tirel?' De Beaumont looked up wearily, and John added, 'I shared his cell before he escaped. I thought him a good man. I just wondered what happened to him.'

De Beaumont considered John a moment longer before answering.

'We searched but could not find him in Winchester, so Prince Henry called things off. He was only locked up because de Breteuil was causing such a fuss, insisting he had proof Tirel plotted to kill the king. However, all those who were there agreed King William the Second's death was a tragic accident. In the end, Henry decided Walter Tirel's escape was the best way to end the matter.'

'Perhaps not his smartest decision,' Barabal said boldly, and de Beaumont raised an eyebrow at her outspoken comment.

'We may be speaking openly here, mistress, but do not take that as licence to say what you please. Calling the future king stupid is not wise any time.'

Barabal had the grace to blush, but she carried on regardless. 'I mean if Walter Tirel is on the loose, and Prince Henry dies before he can be crowned, then he would be a very useful scapegoat.'

'I am not sure that gives de Breteuil a free hand to

murder Prince Henry,' Alain interrupted her. 'If the prince is murdered then Robert Curthose would be the one everyone suspected for both deaths, as he would be the only one to gain from them both. I believe many would only accept him as king if Prince Henry died by natural causes.'

'Prince Henry is a man in his prime and in excellent health. If he dies before being crowned, questions would be raised anyway,' John said.

'But if poisoning could not be proven, their suspicions would remain just that,' de Beaumont added. 'Barons do not like to delve too deeply into things if it is not in their best interests. If there was no obvious sign of foul play, they would be too busy jostling for position to think twice about Prince Henry's death.'

'All this talk gets us nowhere then.' John's exasperation spilled out.

'No, not quite,' Barabal said. 'Stanislaus is in the right place to help us, much though I dislike that we must leave him there.'

'And, in the meantime, we can keep an eye on the prince and anyone serving him,' Alain added. 'It is only two days until the ceremony. He should be safer once that is over.'

De Beaumont stood and stretched.

'Thank you all for your input, but I think what we need now is sleep. There is a tent set up outside for my men. You two boys can find a place to bed down there. I will sleep better myself if you are somewhere safe from de Breteuil's men.

'James will show you the way. Barabal, I will escort you to the ladies' chambers, they should be able to find you somewhere to lie. Tomorrow we shall all need our wits about us. So make sure you all get a good nights rest.'

Before leading Barabal away, Sir Robert de Beaumont ordered one of the servants to find his squire. As James arrived to take them to their quarters, John glanced over his shoulder to find a serving girl knock discreetly on the door to the prince's room. The door opened a crack, and Henry let the smiling girl in.

CHAPTER THIRTEEN
OFF TO LONDON

So exhausted was he from lack of sleep the night before, John was snoring gently the minute his head hit the ground. Moments later, a cold nose pressed to his face, waking him instantly.

Did you forget something?

Oh, Lala, I am so sorry. I was so tired I forgot about you.

I would forgive you, but do you know how dangerous it is for a lamb to be wandering around a camp this size?

Dangerous, are you kidding me? John nearly laughed out loud. *With so many soldiers around, this is the safest place in the kingdom.*

I kid you not. Not everyone sees a cute animal as I wander passed. Some see their next meal.

John stopped laughing. He had not considered Lala to be a source of meat, which would put his life in danger anywhere food was scarce. If anything happened to Lala, not only would he lose a friend, he would also have lost his only chance of getting home. Feeling truly sorry, he opened his swag for the lamb to snuggle beside him.

I am sorry, Lala, I did not think. It will not happen again.

Do not fret, only the body I inhabit would die, but it would have been inconvenient trying to find another way back here. I really must consider these things more carefully in the future.

The lamb curled up and promptly began snoring. John was not so lucky. Sleep now evaded him as thoughts chased each other through his head. *How do you stop someone from poisoning a person? Who was that girl who went into the prince's room? Would Stanislaus be all right? Would he ever get to go home?*

Hours later, snuggling into his swag, unanswerable questions still swirled in his mind as he fell into a restless sleep.

Awoken before dawn the next morning by the noise of breaking camp, John looked blearily over to Alain. Slow to wake, his companion rubbed his eyes as he sat up.

'You boys,' the captain who found them space last night stood over them. 'Roll up your beds, take some bread and a little cheese to break your fast. After, you best go and see to your mounts. We leave at sun up.

'Squire James said you are to ride with us today. So bring your horses back here. Seems you lads cannot be trusted on your own.' Amused, he barked out a laugh before going off to harass someone else.

Muttering under his breath, Alain began rolling up his bedding, and John followed suit with his bedroll.

SWAGMAN

Then the two boys, accompanied by Lala, left the tent to grab some food and small beer from a passing servant before walking over to the stables. With so many people around, John thought it best to pop Lala in his bag, lest he end up in someone's cook pot.

The stable area was crowded, but the boys easily found their tack out by the field where they left their horses the evening before. Surprised de Breteuil had not reclaimed them, they nevertheless readied all three mounts and, leaving Barabal's horse tied to the fence, they led their own back to the camp.

They were early and had to wait while the guards finished packing up. John took the time to watch the others they would journey to London with. Differing uniforms highlighted the number of barons, each with their own retinue, preparing for the day's ride. John realised he had not seen a single noblewoman in the company.

'Where are their wives?' he asked Alain.

'They will be coming by cart, I suppose. If they left yesterday morning, by my estimate they will not arrive in London until tomorrow.'

Question answered, John searched for and found William de Breteuil's men. Stanislaus stood among them and, even though the other boy made a point of ignoring them, it was a relief to see him well and unharmed. John felt a tap on his shoulder and turned to find a tired looking Tom.

'I finally found you. Your friend gave me a message. He said to tell you he is fine, but he needs to speak with you urgently. If he can sneak away when you stop for food at noon, he will tell you then.'

'Thank you, Tom, you have been more than helpful,' John told the young man.

'I hope you did not get into trouble for yesterday,' Alain said.

The boy's face broke into a grin. 'My captain was not happy and I kept waiting for him to give me a punishment. This morning, before we came off duty, your Mistress Barabal turned up to thank the Captain for letting me help you both. I have never seen anyone charm the captain like she did. He tripped over himself, offering to help with anything else she needed in the future. Made me feel quite sick.'

'That is our Barabal,' Alain said in an offhand way.

John turned and considered the boy. He was always complimenting Barabal. Was there something more to their friendship? As if the other boy sensed his interest, he cleared his throat and carried on.

'I am pleased you did not receive any punishment for helping us. Perhaps we can meet again on our way back through to Winchester and share an ale in the tavern.'

'I would like that. I must be off to bed now. I am working again tonight, I am afraid. Safe travels.' Tom waved farewell over his shoulder as he returned to the guard's barracks.

'Speak of the devil,' John said as he caught sight of Barabal leading her horse over to Sir Robert de Beaumont.

She now wore a type of divided skirt so she could ride along with everyone else without showing her legs. James helped her up as the rest of their party mounted. A cart loaded with extra bedding and some of the prince's own servants left the courtyard as more of the barons began to appear. As he moved out of its way, he noticed the pretty serving girl he saw with the prince last night sitting up by the driver.

'Who is she?' John asked Alain, nodding his head at the girl.

The boy turned from glaring at Squire James, who seemed to be taking an extraordinary amount of time getting Barabal settled on her horse, to study the girl John indicated.

'I do not know her. She is not one of the staff from Winchester, and to my knowledge she did not come with the royal party. Prince Henry probably picked her up somewhere. He does that quite a bit I am told.'

Losing interest, he swung his gaze back around to Barabal. John's focus, however, did not waiver. There was something about the girl he did not like. He could not say why, but he thought someone should keep an eye on her. He followed the cart out of town until a commotion by the stables caused him to turn away.

A squire, dressed in de Breteuil's colours, held onto a midnight black stallion, who clearly did not like being around other animals.

'De Breteuil always likes the showy one,' one of the men beside John muttered. 'A pity none of his people can control the beast.'

Horses near the stallion started stamping and shuffling nervously, then the unthinkable happened. The animal jerked his head and the lead rein slipped from the squire's hand. The animal reared up on its hind legs, causing a nearby horse to shuffle to the side, its rider barely able to keep his seat. Another horse bolted back towards the stables, still another bucked and threw his rider to the ground.

'Blast it, boy, what do you think you are doing?' William of Breteuil emerged from behind the building just as his horse's hooves hit the ground and he made ready to rear again. The baron cuffed his charge round the ears and grabbed the reigns before the stallion could make best use of his freedom. 'Get out of my sight, you useless good-for-nothing,' he yelled at the boy as he mounted the beast.

Dropping his head, embarrassed by his master in front of the gathered nobility, the squire went off to find his own mount.

'Poor lad, even the stable master had difficulty with that animal last night,' one of Robert de Beaumont's men commented.

'Not a very forgiving nature for a man of god,' his companion agreed.

The squire came back with his own horse, head still hung low. The noble's behaviour worried John. What if Stanislaus displeased him? Would he receive the same treatment as the squire—or worse?

'Alain, that guard called Sir William de Breteuil "a man of god", that is the second time I have heard someone call him that. What do they mean?'

Already in his saddle, Alain glanced down at John. 'Did you not know? De Breteuil is not only a baron, he is also the Abbot of Breteuil.'

'An abbot? If he is a clergyman he should not be so involved in worldly affairs and politics.' John pondered this new information as he hauled himself into the saddle.

'You do hold some funny ideas.' Alain laughed. 'William was made Abbot of Breteuil because the abbey brings with it a sizeable income. Also the land the monastery sits on gives him considerable influence in the court in Normandie, and here as well.'

'Oh. Is that allowed?' John asked, thinking about the ramshackle house the priest back home lived in, and the time he spent helping poor people in the community.

'If you pay enough money to the right people almost anything is allowed, barring murder. Although, to be truthful, if you pay the right people even that is acceptable.' Alain turned his horse, ready to follow de Beaumont's guards out of Guildford.

John climbed into the saddle and followed his friend, thinking that medieval Briton was nothing at all like the fairy tale his mother read to him.

The long column of nobles did not move as fast as they travelled the day before. Consequently, John found the trip, on the whole, boring. There were only so many fields and small villages you could go through in one day without wishing to see something else.

When they stopped at lunch, he and Alain drifted away and sat, backs against a tree, waiting for Stanislaus to join them. When it became apparent de Breteuil was intent on keeping a close watch on him, they tried to join the group. Any time they wandered near, guards stopped them and turned them away. Only when Stanislaus went to relieve himself behind some bushes and the squire accompanied him, did the boys give up trying to meet with their friends.

Barabal, likewise, was off limits. She sat with the prince's company, eating and laughing, behaving as though she did not have a care in the world.

The girl John worried about served the noon meal, along with the other servants from the cart. Through half closed eyes he spied on her until he realised she did not hand anything directly to Prince Henry. Instead she gave food and drink to a young man sitting nearby, who sampled everything before handing it over to the prince to eat.

'There is not any amount you could pay me to do that job,' John said to Alain.

'He is not paid exactly,' the other boy told him. 'He is a convicted criminal, sentenced to death. He would have been given the option to serve one year as a food taster for the prince, or be hung by the neck. If he survives the year, he earns his freedom and a purse of gold. If the prince dies from poison and he lives, he will be killed and his family will also be sentenced to death. So he chose to do this.'

'Not much of a choice though, is it?' John said, thinking this was just one more example of how barbaric this place was. 'I wonder what type of man would put his family at risk in such a way?'

'A man whose family will not survive for long if he is not around. It is truly a job for the desperate.'

When servants started packing up food, it acted as a signal for everyone else to mount up and continue on to London. John sighed, not looking forward to more hours in the saddle. As a boy, he dreamed of having his own horse and travelling the land. His dream would have been quite different if he had realised how boring and painful it would be.

On the other hand, Alain was terribly excited. He found joy in almost every new place they passed through. John tried not to dampen the boy's spirit, after all, he had never left Winchester before.

When John himself had first heard they were going to London, he too had been eager to go there. His mother always talked about the city as being magnificent, full of wonder and surprises. She had only visited it once on the way to Portsmouth from Northampton, but her time there had given her fond memories. From her description of England's capital city, John had pictured it as a place of excitement and lights and bustle.

The London he came upon at the end of a long day's ride was far different to the one his mother described. As he surveyed the city in the distance, he estimated it might be around the size of Brisbane, which he knew from school had a population of around eighteen thousand people.

Its dwellings clustered around the River Thames, including a large stone tower, a grand church and another palace made of wood. If forced to describe it, he would have said it was grey and smoggy, with not a sparkling light in sight.

'Holy Mother Mary,' Alain whispered in awe. 'Have you ever seen such a huge place? And look, there are King William the Second's masterpieces; The Great Tower, Westminster Cathedral and Westminster Palace. Although it is wrong so much of our taxes were spent to build them, I do feel a certain pride now I see how magnificent they are.'

Secretly, John thought Brisbane was more splendid. But he guessed for the time they were living in, and given the towns and villages they travelled through that day, it was a little impressive. His opinion changed as they road through the streets on the south side of the Thames.

The smell overwhelmed him, and the filth littering the road turned his stomach. This place was a breeding ground for all manner of disease. Alain also wrinkled his nose in distaste, his view of London a little tarnished by this introduction.

As they passed by a group of beggars completely covered in rags, not a piece of skin showing, the column gave them a wide birth. This surprised John as other beggars on their journey had been given some coin, then were moved out of the way.

'What is that about?' John leant over to ask Alain.

'Do you not have lepers where you come from?'

'Lepers?'

'Yes, they have a disease that eats away at the body. It is passed on through touch, so few people want to go near any of the sufferers. I am surprised to find them begging for alms in a city as they tend to live in colonies, hidden away from the general population.'

'Is there no cure?'

'I guess if there are none where you are from there must be, it is just we have not found it yet.'

Soon after, the column came to a wooden bridge, where their progress slowed. The river crossing only took a few horses at a time, and they were at the back of the party. As the sun began to set over the Thames and the buildings of London, John had never felt further from his home.

SWAGMAN

Finally it was their turn to cross the water, and John did so with some trepidation. The gaps between the planks were wide enough for him to see the water rushing below. He marvelled that the gushing tide did not take this flimsy bridge with it. Like many others, he heaved a sigh of relief when he reached the other side safely.

Wearily, de Beaumont's group entered the precinct around Westminster. Many of the other barons and lords had left the group on the way, heading for their London houses. A few barons, including Sir Robert de Beaumont, Sir William de Breteuil, and Ranulf Flambard, elected to stay at the palace with the prince.

Servants appeared from nowhere to take care of the horses and escort everyone to the accommodation prepared for them. Alain spoke to someone and waved for John to follow.

As the servant led them through the grounds through a series of buildings, Alain explained Master Gavin suggested he try to stay with local apothecaries where he could. They were like a brotherhood and would take care of their own.

'Besides, if we stay there, we can stay out of William de Breteuil's way, while still being close to the action,' the boy added.

They followed their guide through to a smaller courtyard containing a cluster of stone buildings. Making for the one on the far end, he lifted the latch and opened the door.

'Master Barwick prefers to stay at his shop unless he is called to the castle for an emergency, but he often has visiting apothecaries staying,' the servant said as he showed them into the dwelling. 'The work room is at the front, and the sleeping room at the back. Old Barwick is particular about his workroom, so I would not touch anything here unless you check with him first. I will ask one of the kitchen staff to tell him you are here when they go to the markets tomorrow.

'Perhaps you would like to take a look around the grounds until I can find a maid with time to bring you fresh linen. Oh yes, there are limited cooking facilities here, so you can take your meals in the kitchen with the staff.'

With those last instructions, the servant left in a rush, no doubt he had a lot of additional work to do with so many people arriving.

John surveyed the ill-kept rooms. The dried herbs hanging from the ceiling sported a thick layer of dust, as did the rows of glass jars arranged neatly on shelves. Even a small stack of books that had fallen over on a work desk under the window cried neglect. In front of them, a well worn work table with benches tucked underneath dominated the room. Behind it, in front of the fireplace, sat two threadbare, but comfortable looking chairs.

Alain entered and headed towards the back door, which led to the bedroom. He opened it to reveal an enormous bed with a rolled up mattress at one end. John joined him, and together they unrolled the pallet.

'What luxury,' Alain exclaimed when they realised the mattress was filled with sheep's wool rather than straw. 'Master Barwick must be a wealthy man if his shop accommodation is better than this.'

John privately thought he and Alain had very different ideas of luxury. His mother would be appalled to think

SWAGMAN

her son slept on anything other than sheep's wool. Before he could voice his opinions though, a knock on the door admitted a maid carrying sheets and blankets.

'I am here to make the bed,' the middle aged woman announced. With her hair escaping her cap, and a blushing red face, she looked more harried than the servant who escorted them here, if that were possible.

'Here, let me take that,' John said as he relieved her of her bundle. 'We can make our own bed,' he told her as he spotted Lala.

Having escaped John's bag, the lamb stared forlornly at the unlit grate.

'If you could send someone to light the fire that will be all we need, thank you.'

The grateful woman thanked them, and quickly departed. Alain and John made the bed and stowed their possessions in the bedroom, then looked at each other.

'Food?' they both said together, and laughed.

Lala, do you want to come with us? John asked.

No, I am fine here. The lamb bedded down on the rushes in front of the fireplace. *I do not think anything of note will happen today, and I have some thinking to do.*

'Come on,' Alain called. 'We want to get something to eat before they start feeding the nobles, otherwise we will have a long wait.'

CHAPTER FOURTEEN
UNCOVERING THE REAL ENEMY

J ohn and Alain exited their quarters into the castle precinct, trying to decide the most likely location of the kitchen.

'Inside?' John asked.

'Are you mad? The palace is made mostly of wood, it would be too dangerous to house a large kitchen inside.' He surveyed the area and pointed to a young boy carrying a basket filled with logs. 'We follow him. That much wood must be for the kitchen fires.'

Shrugging his shoulders, John followed Alain, who followed the boy, who led them round the corner to a stone building that appeared to house the guard quarters. Thinking Alain had made a mistake, he turned and found another stone building behind them, snug up against the wall of the palace. With the double doors thrown wide open, framing two huge fires and showing a number of staff running around preparing food, it had to be the kitchen. He elbowed Alain, and the boy turned with a grin spreading across his face.

The two boys wandered over and looked around, trying to work out where the servants would usually eat. Unable to find what they were looking for, they approached the young boy, who was busy stacking his wood by the fire.

'Can you tell us where the staff table is?' Alain asked, and the boy glanced up, bewildered.

'Whadaya want?'

A voice came from behind and they turned to find a huge man with meaty arms and clothing covered in grease glowering at them. With a wicked looking knife in his hand, and his unwelcoming stare, John was not sure he wanted to answer.

'We are looking for the servant's table,' Alain said, backing up a little from the rather threatening figure.

'Well you asked the wrongun. He cannot hear or speak. You arrived with the prince then?'

When Alain nodded, the cook asked, 'And you are?'

'I am Sir Robert de Beaumont's apothecary, and this is my helper.'

John had to admit he did not sound very convincing.

The man before him raised an eyebrow, folding his arms over his chest.

'Well, of course I am not a full apothecary yet.' The words tumbled out of Alain's mouth as if they had a will of their own. 'But my master trusted me enough to come here in his stead.'

The man laughed and his whole demeanour changed.

'We all start somewhere, lad, and if your master trusts you enough to come here by yourself, then that is good enough for me. Perhaps while you are staying you might take a look at some of the palace staff for us. Just some minor ailments, too small for Master Barwick to bother with now he has moved to town.'

Alain stood taller, changing from the boy he was, to the professional he would become.

'Of course I will. My supply of medicines is only small, but if Master Barwick will let me use some of his stock, I should be able to treat most common ailments.'

'I am sure it will be much appreciated. Now, I must return to my meat. It would not do to let anything burn with our guests being who they are. Take a seat and someone will bring food by-the-by.'

John started through the door the cook indicated, and found himself in a room filled with a square wooden table. Twenty people would comfortably find seating on the benches tucked beneath. On the other side of the table the wall was broken by another door.

'So staff can come and go as they are called to serve,' Alain explained. 'It will lead to the palace proper.'

As they were the first people to arrive for supper, it felt strange sitting alone at one end of such a huge table waiting to be served. They had not been seated long when a kitchen hand rushed in, dropped some wooden bowls in front of them, and rushed out again. He returned with two pitchers filled with ale, spilling liquid on the table as he plunked them down beside some wooden cups, before bustling out.

John's mouth watered at the smells coming from the

kitchen, but the boy did not return with food. They waited patiently, but no one brought them anything to put on the plates they had liberated from the stack. Alain had risen to go and find out what caused the delay, when the door from the palace opened.

Sitting back down, the two boys watched as the servants from Winchester who travelled with them to London entered and arranged themselves around the other end of the table. No one spoke. Silently they each took a plate from the stack, and one of them filled cups of small beer from the jugs or their group. They did not so much as acknowledge the boys. Alain glanced at John and smirked, ready to have some fun.

'So, Tobias, you wrangled yourself a trip to London.'

One of the oldest of the group peered down his nose at Alain, then turned away as if it was beneath him to answer the boy.

'In Winchester he ate with the servants in the hall. How it must gall him to be forced to eat in here with us. They will probably expect him to serve the nobility later. That will put him in his place,' Alain whispered to John.

'Mmm,' John answered, too distracted by the girl who slipped into Prince Henry's room the night before to pay full attention to Alain and his teasing.

As he regarded her, he caught her glancing back at him and Alain, trying not to be seen to be doing so. Her eyes met his as she reached for a drink, and he jerked back in surprise at the hatred they contained.

He wondered what he had done to earn that sort of response from a complete stranger. Before he could tell Alain, his attention wavered as a platter piled with steaming hot meat, and bread warm from the oven, was placed in front of him. His stomach's need took over and John pushed all thoughts of the strange girl to the back of his mind. Later, as he left the table, John tried to remember the last time his stomach had been this full, and could not.

'Agh, my stomach is like a drum. Maybe we should have a bit of a walk before heading back,' John suggested. 'Perhaps we will run into Stanislaus or Barabal and find out what they are up to.'

'They will be eating with the great of the land in the dining hall. We might take a wander past there on the way back,' Alain conceded.

They left the servant's dining room by the door into the palace. As they did, someone tightly gripped John's arm, pulling him backwards. He turned to find the girl glaring at him with such intense hatred he took a step back. Her grip tightened and her fingers dug into his arm.

'Tell your guardian to stay away. This one is already lost. If you continue to thwart me, I will make it my mission to ensure you and your guardian never leave this time.' She abruptly released his arm, turned on her heel and stalked off towards the hall.

Alain, realising John had not followed, turned around and stared in confusion as the serving girl passed him.

'What did she want?' Alain's eyes automatically followed the attractive servant as she strode away.

'I am not sure,' John said. 'I am pretty certain she just threatened me. We need to talk with Lala before we catch up with the others.'

SWAGMAN

And you are sure she is not part of the Winchester staff?
Lala asked Alain again.

I told you, I never saw her before today, Alain answered,
his tone petulant as he repeated himself.

I found her entering the prince's room last night, John
said. *Then I saw her with the other staff from Guildford
today, attending to the prince and his group.*

This is not good. Lala paced the room.

Why not? Do you not understand what she said?

Worried by the lamb's tone of voice, John knew the
answer was going to be something he would not like.
Lala did not answer immediately, which concerned John
even more. Ignoring them, the lamb paced around the
room for some time, before coming to a stop in front of
the two boys.

*With the unplanned turn of events around King William's
death, we had not expected them to be here. At the very
least, we did not think they would arrive so fast. Especially
as in the grand scheme of things, this was such a small
change to the course of history. The second King William
would have died next month of a heart attack, so Prince
Henry will only be taking the crown a month early.* Lala
paused before continuing.

*I chose Henry's coronation as my first solo assignment
purely because it should have been simple. Free from
outside interference. Mmm, maybe it is not that they arrived
so quickly, maybe they were here before us. That would*

explain it. Why did no one notice and send me a warning? Lala pondered out loud.

Lala, who are they? John's exasperation at Lala's meanderings came through loud and clear.

They do not have a name as such, we call them the Time Wreckers. Lala sighed in John's head. *The universe must be in balance. Where there is good, there is evil. Where forces work to bring about harmony and progress in the world, forces working for chaos and regression will also be found. I believe your maid is one of them, one of the wreckers.*

John let loose with a string of curses that would have been right at home in a shearing shed. When he calmed down, he glared at the lamb in front of him and spoke his frustrations out loud.

'You bring me here with next to no information, to make sure something totally out of my control happens, forgetting to tell me this is your first solo mission. Now you inform me all along we had some other organisation working against us, trying to prevent Prince Henry from becoming king. Have you forgotten to let me know about anything else?'

Some part of John was aware Alain stared, opened mouthed, trying to take in what was happening between John and the Time Guardian. However, with all his energy focused on trying to deal with everything he had learnt today, John did not have the capacity to help his friend deal with this.

There is one positive thing to come out of this encounter. Lala's tone was conciliatory.

'Really? It had better be good, because at the moment

SWAGMAN

I do not see how we can stop both the forces of chaos and a noble intent on Prince Henry's death, when we cannot even access two of our helpers to warn them of this new development,' John spat out at the lamb, his anger still not yet under control.

The universe places limitations on how we are able to affect events in other times, the lamb offered. *We cannot just turn up and kill someone to make sure an event does or does not go ahead. We also cannot initiate some new course of action a person from the time has not thought of themselves. All we are capable of doing is ensuring an existing plan moves things in the right direction.*

John paced the room, trying to digest this new information.

'Let me get this straight. Neither she nor I can take any direct action against a person in this time, we have to work with the people from here. That is why I am with Alain, Barabal and Stanislaus. So, it stands to reason she is working with someone else too.'

I believe so, or at the very least, she is searching for someone to work with.

John's thoughts were spinning out of control, and he was having difficulty wrangling them into a logical pattern. A random thought popped into his mind then out of his mouth before he could stop it.

'Hold on, what about when Alain and Stanislaus broke me out of prison and released Walter Tirel. In the other time line, did he escape?'

No, because in the original timeline Walter Tirel never shot an arrow at the king. The hunt was successful and King William the Second held his barons' court, imposing another tax levy. The barons did not take the additional monetary burden well. The stress this placed on King William, combined with the worry of trying to squeeze blood from a stone to keep his court running, placed too much strain on his heart. The fact he over-indulged his appetite cannot have helped either.

Lala froze, cocked his head to the side, then carried on. *Now I think on it, Time Wreckers may have worked to ensure Tirel's arrow hit the king, and they may also have been behind his capture. If they succeeded in having him tried for murder, and were able to link everything to Prince Henry, Robert Curthose would be crowned king unopposed.*

The funny thing is universal balance will be maintained, come what may. If they interfered beyond their remit, then the universe would work to rebalance everything. So it was perhaps no coincidence you were in Walter's cell, and that he escaped when you did.

John continued pacing until he calmed down, and things started to fit together in his mind.

'How could they make sure Tirel's arrow hit the king?'

Lala did not answer, he simply stared at John, as if saying "look at me".

'Ah, they could have taken the form of a stag and set everything up.'

Yes, that is certainly one possibility.

'All right, so they would have acted directly and put things out of balance. If I do something other than help, the universe will do something to place things back in balance too?'

Of course. That is why I counselled you to keep quiet and let things take their own course. I wonder if the

*universe conspired to have you and Tirel share a cell, and
then be released together to realign things.*

John thought some more, and paced some more, and
then stopped in the middle of the room. Thoughts were still
chasing each other inside his head, refusing to be tamed
into a useful pattern. He was aware time was running out,
so they needed to focus on things they were able to do.

'This Time Wrecker is likely to be working with someone
else,' John said.

*That is possible. And, if she is working with someone,
we need to find out who.*

'I believe we already know who it is. If Walter Tirel
never killed the king, it is likely the person who captured
him and proposed the idea of a conspiracy is the one
working with the Time Wreckers.'

Pieces began falling into place for John, much like
the old jigsaw he and his brothers used to put together.

That is as good a place to start as any.

'Well, Walter Tirel told me it was de Breteuil who lay
in wait for him when he returned to get what he needed
to escape the country. I think it is safe to assume he is
part of the same plot. Now we know who is behind
everything, and who is going to administer the poison.'

'How did you make that leap?' Alain had closed his
mouth and now tried to follow John's deductive reasoning.

'Prince Henry has an eye for pretty ladies and I saw
that serving girl slip into his room last night, and none
of the guards stopped her to check her over. What better
way to by-pass the Prince's food tasters than using the
woman warming his bed?'

Alain stared into the distance for a moment, brow

furrowed in thought, then asked, 'Did you see her take in any food with her last night? Or witness the prince taking anything directly from her hand today?'

John considered the question for a moment, then shook his head. 'I am quite sure she had nothing with her yesterday, and she would not be foolish enough to feed poison to the prince in plain sight. I think we need to stop her from taking anything into the prince's room tonight.'

John felt much better knowing their task was not insurmountable. He and Alain needed to figure out how to watch the prince's bedroom without being moved on by his guards. As he pondered this question, the door to their rooms flung open and Stanislaus barged through.

'I have it,' he told them, his face breaking into a grin. 'De Breteuil bought poison in Guildford and a serving girl is willing to give it to the prince. She is biding her time, earning his trust, so she can slip it into his food when she joins him tonight.'

'We know,' Alain responded for them all, and Stanislaus' expression turned from pleased to crestfallen.

'If you knew, why did you make me stay with that prat?'

'We only just now realised, literally moments before you arrived,' Alain said. 'The serving girl gave herself away, and we only now worked out she is in league with de Breteuil. If she had not slipped up, you would have been the only one who knew.' Alain mollified his friend, and John could see Stanislaus perk up. 'At least now we know you do not need to return to de Breteuil's rooms.'

At that, Stanislaus looked sheepish. 'I could not go back anyway. I am afraid I broke and told him on reflection I thought Prince Henry would make a better king than

Robert Curthose. I mean, the man he thinks would be the best ruler for Briton is dull as dishwater. He has not got an original thought in his head. My father despises the man. De Breteuil turned beetroot red and told me to get out and never darken his door again.'

'Well, now we know what is happening, you are better off being as far away from that man as possible.' Alain reassured his friend. 'You are welcome to bunk here with us, or I am sure Sir Robert de Beaumont would be pleased if you returned to his service. We explained to him you had not actually joined with de Breteuil, but were spying for us. I am sure if you tell him what you told us, you will be welcomed back as the hero you are.'

How else were we going to explain how we made the connection? Alain responded to John's unasked question as they left the room in search of de Beaumont. *I cannot see the prince or Sir Robert de Beaumont believing in guardians and time travel, no matter how enlightened they both are.*

Barabal moved the food from her plate to her mouth without being aware of what she was eating, so intently was she watching the action at the top table. The serving girl she had taken the wine from last night was paying far too much attention to Prince Henry, and for some unknown reason that annoyed her.

It was not that she wished herself in the girl's place, attracting the attention of the future king for her own ends, Barabal considered that the wrong type of recognition. Although from birth girls were drilled to believe looks were important to attract a husband of the right type, no matter how beautiful a girl was she could not marry above her station. A prince would never marry someone who served him. Which meant the girl must be trying to attract his attention for other reasons.

What could the girl gain from a relationship with a prince? Prince Henry had a wandering eye, but he also had a reputation for leaving behind broken hearts, and often children in his wake. Lower bred mothers were paid off, and left in positions where they were despised by the other staff. It was only the women of noble birth who were looked after, and their offspring raised as nobles.

Sighing, Barabal admitted she was a little jealous of the regard that particular serving girl received from the males in the room. Everyone from boys to old men followed her figure with longing gazes. Although she knew her own features to be pleasing, with dark brown eyes set in an oval face all framed by wavy brown hair, it was her body that did not attract the eye. Her petite, slim frame, showed little promise of gaining curves as she moved into womanhood, and would never be able to compete with someone like the maid.

Not only did the serving girl have midnight black hair and startling blue eyes set in the face of an angel, she also had all the right curves in all the right places. As she moved through a room, men stopped what they were doing and followed her with their eyes.

She shook the dark thoughts from her head. No use worrying over something you could not change. Instead

SWAGMAN

she decided she may as well try and figure out what about the girl made her feel uneasy. What would she gain from this type of attention?

Leaning her head on her hand as she studied the girl, she earned a sharp reprimand for poor table manners from the lady sitting next her. Biting back a retort about how silly it was to worry about elbows on the table lest her bad manners be reported back to Sir Robert de Beaumont, she realised the object of her scrutiny no longer stood behind the prince. A scan of the room confirmed she had disappeared.

Politely excusing herself from the table, she slipped through the hall's side door. Upon finding the corridor empty, she quietly tiptoed down towards the entranceway. Peeking around the corner she found it empty. Drawing her head back, she caught a movement over by the door to the servant's dining hall. While wondering how she might get closer to overhear the conversation, her eye was drawn by a movement.

Risking a quick look around the corner again, she observed de Breteuil calmly walking out from the shadows. As he returned to dine, he did not so much as even glance her way. Still unnoticed, she decided to wait and find out who he was talking to. Her patience was rewarded with the sight of the maid entering the servant's dining room and shutting the door behind her.

Well, how interesting. All the pieces tumbling round in her head fell into place. That was how Sir William de Breteuil would gain access to poison the prince. Smiling to herself, she could not wait to let the boys in on her triumph.

CHAPTER FIFTEEN
STALKING THE PRINCE

The three boys rushed to the dining hall, only to find they need not have hurried as the court had not long started dinner. Peeking through the door, they found Barabal sitting with some of the other palace women looking completely bored. Catching sight of her friends, she excused herself and exited the hall.

'You all took your time.' She grabbed Stanislaus by the arm and led them out into the courtyard where they could speak without being overheard. 'I have been waiting ages for you to come and find me. I think one of the serving girls is up to something. I caught her talking with William de Breteuil earlier. I want you to follow her and find out if she is in on their plot.'

'The dark haired one? She is, de Breteuil is plotting with her to poison Prince Henry before the coronation,'

SWAGMAN

Stanislaus told her, pride sounding in his voice. 'I overheard them talking.'

Barabal's mouth formed an "O". 'You know already.' Deflated, she was quick to recover her poise as she instructed them, 'We need to stop her.'

'Of course we do,' Alain said. 'But how?'

'We should knock her over the head, tie her up and stick her somewhere,' Stanislaus announced.

His three companions glared at him, but the boy did not back down.

'It might not be the best plan, but it is a plan. And it will be pretty effective.'

Although he had some ideas of how they should proceed, John remembered what Lala said, and he decided the others should be left to come up with a way forward themselves.

'The wench wormed her way into Prince Henry's bed to gain access to kill him. Barabal, maybe you can oust her. You would be better for Prince Henry anyway.' Stanislaus' second plan was met with the same, if not more, disdain than his first.

'Are you mad?' Barabal's body tensed with suppressed anger. 'Is that all you think a woman is good for? Warming a man's bed? And do you think so little of me that you would ask me to use my body in that way?'

Rising anger caused her to run out of words, so she settled for clenching her fist and punching Stanislaus right in the stomach. The boy doubled over, looking sorry for himself.

'Barabal, my apologies, I did not think. Of course I would not want you to become Prince Henry's mistress, well, not unless you wanted to. You are worth more than that. I thought maybe he might fall in love with you and take you for his queen. You would be such a great queen.'

In the face of Stanislaus' boyish romanticism, Barabal's anger washed away.

'Oh, Stanislaus, you numbskull. Prince Henry brokered a marriage with Princess Edith. And even if he were not betrothed, he would never marry anyone as low born as me. Besides, when I wed, it will be to someone who treats me as an equal, not as something pretty to hang off their arm. I hope one of you can come up with a better plan.'

Directing her comments to Alain and John, she waited for them to answer. Alain remained thoughtful, but said nothing. It was left to John to outline the plan he and Alain discussed earlier. However, before he had a chance, Stanislaus showed he was not yet done.

'Why do we not just tell de Beaumont? He would then be able to keep the prince safe and we could enjoy the festivities.'

Barabal at least did him the courtesy of thinking his idea through before dismissing it, which showed John how much the girl thought of the squire.

'Stanislaus you were not there when Sir Robert de Beaumont assured us the prince had enough safeguards to prevent him from being poisoned. I really do not believe he will change his mind and talk to the prince. I can already hear him saying speculation is not evidence.'

Even though Barabal let the squire down gently this time, he still slumped his shoulders in defeat. John decided now was the best time to offer their alternative idea.

'Alain and I discussed this before, and we believe we

only need to make sure the serving girl takes no food or drink into the room when she goes to meet with Prince Henry in private.'

'Sounds easy enough.' Barabal nodded. 'I think we can use an alcove not far from the prince's bedroom. If we watch the room, we can stop her from entering with anything in her hands.

'We will take turns. John, you and I will take the first watch after dinner. Alain, you and Stanislaus will relieve us after the three am bell is rung.

'Right, I best get back to the meal. I can make sure he eats nothing the others do not while I am around. John, wait outside the door and join me once the meal is over.'

Orders issued, Barabal swept past them and returned to the dining hall, not even pausing to check they agreed with her plan.

'I am off to find some food, then to see if I can bunk in with James tonight,' Stanislaus told them, happy to be free from Sir William de Breteuil's clutches. 'Alain, come wake me at three.'

'I will need to, because you sleep like a log and will never hear the bell,' Alain said under his breath as his friend walked away. 'Wait up, Stanislaus, I might join you for some more supper. See you after three,' he called back over his shoulder to John.

With everyone else having something to do, John found

himself at a loose end. Casually kicking at a loose tile, he decided he may as well wait for Barabal closer to the action. Snooping through the door he saw serving staff lined around the wall, waiting for instructions.

Guessing with this many new people no one would notice an additional face, he slipped into the room and made his way to a gap behind Barabal. The only sign she noticed his entrance was the way she deliberately glanced away as he neared her table.

After a short time, John's legs began to cramp from standing still for so long. He shuffled from foot to foot, while trying to keep an eye on the room. Compared to everyone else, de Breteuil and his retinue were sombre. Once again they were not seated at the top table, a sign of disfavour for someone so high born, or so he gathered from the comments the boy beside him made when he caught John watching the nobleman. Given his objections to Prince Henry taking the crown of Briton, he understood the apparent demotion, but he did not share this with his informant.

Surveying the top table, he managed to catch de Beaumont's eye. The Baron tilted his head in acknowledgement, and returned to his conversation. However, John still could not find the one person he was looking for.

As servants placed yet another course of food on the tables, he finally found his target. The girl busied herself serving the prince, making a point of not serving Prince Henry himself, but placing the dish of steaming fish down in front of the poor condemned man to test before the prince ate. Almost as though she felt John's gaze, she raised her head and sent a look that could only be read as a challenge in his direction.

'Pretty, that Isolde, isn't she? I suggest you stay away from her though. All her time is spent trying to catch a prince, and she won't let anything get in her way,' his servant friend murmured.

John responded by shuffling his feet again, wondering just how long this meal would take.

'New to this?' his companion asked. 'There are still two more courses to go. It helps if you stand one foot flat, use the toes of the other foot to balance, then two feet, then the other foot. You will not fidget so much that way.'

'Thank you,' John whispered, and tried following his suggestion. Although still tiring, it was decidedly easier on his legs. Even so, his feet were nearly numb by the time the prince stood and ended the meal.

John slipped in behind Barabal as she left. The girl led them down the corridor to the sleeping quarters. When he caught her up, she was speaking to de Beaumont. She was explaining she needed an excuse to be gone from the women's quarters for the evening, an excuse that would not tarnish her reputation. De Beaumont thought for a moment before he responded.

'Perhaps I could take ill and send you to Master Barwick for a remedy. John and Squire James can accompany you. I will send James along to bring Master Barwick regardless. If something actually does happen to the prince, it would be best for a trained apothecary to be on hand. If he is not poisoned, I am sure Prince Henry would welcome him at the coronation tomorrow.'

'Excellent thinking, thank you, sir. Come, John, let us take our position for the night.'

'You told de Beaumont about the poison. I thought we were not going to?' he whispered as they left the baron behind.

'I had to tell him why I needed to be out tonight didn't I?' She said no more, clearly not feeling the need to explain herself any further.

Turning down another hallway, Barabal pointed to an alcove with a table.

'It is where the maids place dishes and bedding and the like when serving this far away from the kitchen and laundry,' Barabal explained. 'Here, give me a hand.'

John helped her move the furniture back into the corner. This made enough room for one person to sit on the table and another to stand beside without being seen, unless you specifically looked into the space.

They started with John sitting and Barabal standing, because she said she was too full after her evening meal to sit comfortably. They swapped places some time later. Then changed again, and once more, before anyone came down the corridor.

Remaining statue still as the prince passed by, flanked by two men and followed by two guards, the pair only relaxed when the group stopped by the prince's door. John knew Ranulf Flambard, but not the other man who wore the robes of a cleric.

'Archbishop Anslem,' Barabal mouthed.

'Everything is ready for the coronation in the abbey tomorrow,' the cleric told the prince. 'However I shall need the document containing your written promises to the church before we proceed.'

'My scribes are working on the final copy now. When

SWAGMAN

I checked earlier today, they assured me they would be finished tomorrow morning. There will be ample time to peruse it before you place the crown on my head in the afternoon.

'Now Ranulf will escort you out, I need to get some sleep before meeting with the barons early tomorrow. They too want to finalise our agreement before the ceremony.'

The prince's tone was firm but polite, and John had noted a weariness around his eyes as he passed their hiding place. Three days of travelling took its toll on a person, and no doubt the prince had been working late into the night as well. John sympathised as he stifled his own yawn.

'Your Highness.'

The cleric bobbed his head as the prince opened the door to his room and closed it behind himself, ensuring the meeting ended.

'He is true to his word?' the archbishop asked Ranulf.

'Yes, I checked the document myself, and everything you asked for is included. He is perhaps the only one of William the Conqueror's spawn you can actually trust.'

'Perfect. Shall we seal this with some more wine?'

No sooner had their voices faded than new footsteps echoed down the corridor. They were lighter and quieter, and John guessed they belonged to a female. He confirmed his suspicions when he stepped out into the path of Isolde. Barabal moved in behind the girl, trapping her between them.

'More wine for the prince, I see.' Barabal spoke in her most polite, reasonable voice, the one John knew meant she was deadly serious. 'I think perhaps this is another pitcher I need to take from you, for very different reasons.'

'Just try it,' the girl sneered. 'I shall scream the place down and we will find out how Prince Henry deals with those who accost his favoured servant.'

'Go ahead,' John told her. 'I for one would be interested in his reactions when we tell him the wine you brought for your cosy evening together is poisoned.'

John had no way of knowing whether or not this actual jug of wine contained poison intended for Prince Henry, but, given the circumstances, he was happy to bluff. Isolde stared at him, weighing her options. Grudgingly she handed over the pitcher, and slipped past John. She took a single step, then turned.

'You cannot protect him all the time. You will make a mistake, and I will succeed.'

'We do not need to watch him every minute,' Barabal said as she slipped back into the alcove. 'We only need to be on the lookout when he has time to spend alone with you, and he will have little enough of that before he is crowned tomorrow.'

Isolde did not rise to the bait, instead she carried on towards her destination as though nothing had happened, tapped on the door, and the prince admitted her into his bedroom. John carried the pitcher over to an open window and poured the contents out. Placing the empty jug at the back of the table, he once again took up his position.

No one else used the corridor for some time, so they took turns napping until they were disturbed by thumping and laughing. A bleary-eyed Alain, followed by a still half-asleep Stanislaus, appeared in front of them.

'You look terrible,' Barabal told the boys. 'Even worse

than we do, and we have not had any sleep.'

'Nor have I,' Alain said. 'I woke at every bell, worried I might miss out hearing the three am one.'

'I slept fine, well until Alain came into my room and woke me,' Stanislaus cheerfully informed them. 'You had wine to drink? Alain, why did we not think of bring some with us?'

'No, you dolt, we took a pitcher from the serving wench. She is in with Prince Henry now,' Barabal informed them.

'Oh.' Stanislaus was crestfallen.

'I can test the dregs tomorrow if you can take the pitcher back with you, John,' Alain said as he peered into the jug to see how much liquid was left.

'Well, I am off to bed. See you later.' Barabal slipped off the table and waited for John to follow.

He picked up the wine jug and slowly dragged his body down the corridor and out into the palace precinct. Finding the door to his quarters he opened it to find an elderly man sitting in one of the chairs by the fire, with Lala standing in front of him.

'You are correct Great One, he is not much to look at, but you must work with what you are given,' the man said to the lamb. 'Come in and close the door, boy, no use letting all the warm air out. These old bones do tend to feel the cold a little more nowadays.'

John shut the door behind him, his tired brain trying to work out who this strange man talking to his guardian was. As he placed the jug down and walked over to the chairs, his over-worked memory dredged up the answer.

'You are Master Barwick. Sir Robert de Beaumont said he would send Squire James for you.' John sunk into the other chair, pleased with his guess, and happy with the way the evening had gone.

'Of course,' the rather portly, well dressed man confirmed, his blue eyes twinkling. 'Your guardian was just bringing me up to date with progress so far.'

John studied the man through half-closed eyes, thinking Master Barwick was nothing like he imagined when the cook had been complaining about the apothecary not tending to their illnesses. In his mind he had envisioned a thin, sour skinflint, not this kindly looking grandfather figure with white hair standing out in clumps from his head.

'Cook is right to complain. I used to tend the people here. When I became less mobile, I sent my apprentice down. Last fall he became a journeyman and set up his own business north of London. I do not venture out much nowadays, and I cannot summon the energy to train another to service the people here. I am so pleased your friend offered to help as the castle staff no doubt suffered because of my neglect. As I am here now, I may even stay a few extra days and give what assistance I can.'

'Did you read my mind?' Now wide awake and on his guard, John sat upright and glared suspiciously at the newcomer.

Master Barwick frowned, 'Why yes, did your guardian not tell you? Many guardian's assistants can tell what others are thinking.'

SWAGMAN

John stared at Lala. *What have you withheld from me now?*

'Oh, I pick up mind speaking too,' the man laughed. 'Not much can be kept from me.'

Master Barwick is a candidate for guardian. Each generation produces a person ready to be elevated to one of the twenty-four. He has special skills, and he knew when we arrived in London. I asked him to come here when I realised Prince Henry might be poisoned. When James knocked at his door this evening, he was prepared and ready to travel.

'And you did not think to tell me about him?' John asked.

You did not come back til now. How could I?

'Oh, I guess you could not really.' John had to concede the point to Lala.

'So they tried tonight?' Master Barwick asked. 'You stopped them though, good lad.'

'I really wish you would stop doing that,' John grumbled. 'As it turns out, we intercepted some wine, but except for drinking it ourselves, we have no way of knowing whether or not it was poisoned. Alain said he will try and find out tomorrow.'

'If you do not like people reading you, you need to learn to put up some walls. Honestly, Sigma, that should be the first thing you teach them. He must be broadcasting your plans to anyone with a little talent.'

I misjudged our entry a little, so training time has been limited.

'Sigma? Is that your name?'

Not my real name, my guardian name. We are all named after a letter from the Greek alphabet.

'Well, I think Lala suits you at the moment, so I shall continue to call you that. Can you really teach me to shield my thoughts?'

Yes, I can, and I will. Just not now. You are tired and should sleep. You need to be alert tomorrow, and it would not do for you to fall asleep while you protect a future king.

Feeling like a young boy sent to bed, none-the-less John admitted he could do with a decent night's sleep, so did not argue. Wishing the others goodnight, he went next door, undressed and slipped into the bed still a little warm from where Alain had lain.

After John left them alone again, Master Barwick turned his attention back to the lamb in front of him.

Sigma, are you certain this is the one who is going to save the timeline? A bit on the green side, in my opinion, and I cannot imagine his friends are seasoned fighters.

I was worried as well, Lala told the man in front of him. *But I found all the required signs; the beginnings of magical ability, a need to do what is right, and a stout heart. Circumstances forced me to bring him from earlier in his evolution than was optimal, but you know how the council likes us to solve two problems with one event. The time I took him from was the one in his circle of life that he would most benefit from learning about the Charter of Liberties, and what it took for the document to be produced.*

This devolution of power, and the resulting belief all

SWAGMAN

people have some rights, are the lynchpin of the shearers strike in the far off land I took him from. Also, there is a lesson he needs to learn to be able to temper the radicals in his era to bring about real change.

I guess if the council approved it, this must be the right course of action. He just seems so young, and so impetuous, the apothecary commented.

As am I by Guardian standards. Lala sighed. *I guess we are well matched. Although, I was a bit surprised when he got himself thrown in the dungeon. That almost ruined my plans. Funnily enough though, it galvanised the team so it worked out well in the end.*

And do you think they will be able to combat a Time Wrecker now that we know they are here? It sounds as though they sent a seasoned operative, and I am afraid I am not mobile enough to be of much use to them. Master Barwick worried.

It is the one they sent that concerns me the most. I felt none of the ripples normally accompanying their arrival. The council did not know of a Time Wrecker present in this time either. I am afraid our enemy sent one of their best to deal with this situation. The lamb's face contorted in what Master Barwick took to be a frown.

I hope you have this under control, Sigma. I must come back to this time once our next mission is complete, and I do not want to return to chaos. At my age, I want life to become easier, not harder.

It will all turn out well, I am sure. And if it does not, you will not be back here for long. I sense the end of your natural life will be soon. Once your body passes on, your training as a guardian will begin. Anyway, I am confident we will thwart the wreckers' agent.

Although the lamb sounded unconcerned about how the wreckers might affect the time line, Sigma was unable to totally shield his fear from the elderly man. However, realising there was nothing else they could do now, Master Barwick decided to change the subject.

I guess I should trust you, and we both should trust in the Council. Have you heard any more from them about what is in store for us when your mission here is complete?

We will meet with them tonight, in fact, I hear them calling now.

CHAPTER SIXTEEN
THE PLOT THICKENS

John awoke the next morning to the sound of laughter next door. He stumbled about pulling on his clothes so he could find the source of the disruption. He found Alain and Master Barwick sitting on one side of the work table, and the meat cook sitting on the other.

'So my friend, my lame foot will not support my weight any more. The less I walk, the more weight I put on, with more weight, I can walk less. For me to even ride a horse now is difficult.'

'I wish you had told us. Your apprentice did not explain to us why he came instead of you. Sour puss that one. We were pleased to see the back of him,' Cook said before taking a sip of water. Thirst quenched, he continued, 'Anyway, we thought we were beneath you now you have a fancy place in town. If we had known about your condition, we would have sent the cart for you. We still can, and you could come down once a week like you used to. Join us for a hearty meal and some wine; catch up with your friends.'

No longer angry with the apothecary, cook welcomed his old mate back to the fold, and Master Barwick seemed pleased to be included once again.

'Now that would be grand. It gets lonely in my shop, only seeing those with ailments. So, shall we find out where Alain is with his learning. Boy, cook here has a sore back, it has been giving him pain for years, too much standing and lifting all those heavy carcasses. What would you recommend?'

John decided he best leave the others to their work, and crossed the floor to find Lala sound asleep. Thinking it likely the lamb and Master Barwick talked through the night, he decided to let the guardian rest and go feed his grumbling stomach. He took himself off to the servant's dining room, where he found Stanislaus wolfing down porridge with honey and nuts.

'Morning.' The other boy greeted him through a mouthful of food.

John helped himself to a bowl of steaming oatmeal and sat down beside his friend. 'Did anything else happen after we left last night?'

'Not really. The girl left before sun up. Glared at us as she walked past, saucy wench. Nothing else happened until Prince Henry went to breakfast. Sir Robert de Beaumont will be with him until the midday meal, sorting out a heap of documents, then Barabal said you guys would take over and watch until the ceremony.

SWAGMAN

'I am finishing up here, then I am off back to bed.' Stanislaus stretched and yawned before continuing to empty his plate.

Not wanting to spend the morning alone, John asked, 'Do you want to take a wander with me first? I need to find out if the wine we discarded last night killed anything.'

'I thought Alain was going to test the pitcher?'

'He is so caught up with Master Barwick and tending to castle staff's ailments, I doubt there will be time for him to do it before this afternoon's festivities begin.'

Stanislaus shrugged. 'All right. Although I am not sure what you expect to find.'

'Nor am I, but I will know it when I see it,' John admitted.

After returning their plates into the kitchen, they walked around, attempting to count windows to find the spot where John emptied the jug the previous night. The precinct was busy, and a couple of times they had to lie, saying they were on a mission for the prince, lest they be hauled into preparations for the celebrations.

Frustrated because the outside of the palace looked different to the inside, John was about to suggest Stanislaus go in, find the window and lean out, when the other boy stopped dead in his tracks and pointed. In one of the garden beds, a pile of dead rats spilled out on to the pathway. They might have been killed by anything, except there was a red wine stain on one of the stones beside the bodies.

'Well, don't just stand there, boys, clean that mess up.'

A gardener pushed a basket and shovel at Stanislaus, who promptly dropped them and ran.

'Oops, I forgot, I am meant to be serving Sir Robert de Beaumont this morning, he will be annoyed with me if I am late,' he shouted back over his shoulder as he disappeared into the crowd.

With the gardener staring intently at him, John had no alternative but to pick up the spade and begin shovelling rodents.

'Odd this is, never seen so many dead rats in one place. They do like to rummage in the garden manure, so I find an occasional one when I am working. But this? I have not seen anything like it in all my years working here.'

After John finished, the man directed him to the dung heap, telling him to bury the dead rats deep down. As John left, he busied himself tidying the garden so no trace of the dead rodents would be visible to the gathering nobility. Job completed, John found himself with nothing to do until the noon meal.

He entered the palace through the servant's entrance and lurked in the hall. One of the maids told him Mistress Barabal attended the women of the household, working on the prince's coronation robes. John happened to mention Barabal might prefer to come explore London with him rather than spending such a beautiful morning sewing, and earned a cuff to the side of the head for his observations.

Sighing, he left the palace and made his way down to the Thames. The morning sun reflected on the muddy blue water, causing the tips of the waves to sparkle as the tide went out. Criss-crossing the river, boats brought produce to feed the population of the large city.

John sat on the bank, dangling his legs over. As he swung them back and forth, he gazed around the town he could only describe as grey, missing the reds and blues that reminded him of his Queensland home. As he sat wallowing in his homesickness, his eyes found a boat heading for Westminster dock. Idly he followed its progress, and as it drew closer, he realised he knew the passengers; Sir William de Breteuil and Isolde the maid.

Searching the dock area, he found some wooden crates stacked nearby. Trying to act casual, he walked over to them and secreted himself in behind, hoping to overhear a little of the conversation as the two passed him by. Luck must have been on his side that day, as the pair stopped by the crates to finish their conversation.

'I say killing him now is too risky. If those blasted children are on to you, we should cut our losses and give up the plan.' De Breteuil's tone was commanding.

'The risk is not with you,' the persuasive purr belonged to Isolde. 'They will look for me once the prince is dead, and I intend on being a long way from here when they find his body. That is, if they even realise he was poisoned. No one of importance has seen you and I together. Your reputation will be safe.'

De Breteuil grunted, not used to having his decisions questioned. Still, he did not walk away. Fingers tapped a rhythm on the wooden crate as the duke considered the servant's words.

'I am not sure.' The duke's tone was uncertain when he answered.

'Just tell me you still want Prince Henry poisoned, and I will do my best to see the job done. There is still enough of the tonic for one more attempt.' Isolde pushed her accomplice, not yet ready to give in.

'I do, damn it,' de Breteuil told her.

'Consider it done. I must away now before someone

notices I am gone.'

A rustle of skirts was followed a few moments later by the thud of heavier footsteps. John popped his head over the top of the crates to glimpse de Breteuil's retreating back.

He slumped down again, back against the crates. Annoyingly he had not learnt anything new from the conversation, except de Breteuil's resolve wavered, but not enough to prevent Isolde from bringing him back into line.

Time was running out. And with only enough poison left for one last attack, this afternoon would be her last opportunity to try anything. Sighing, he stood and headed back to the apothecary's, hoping to talk to Lala and Master Barwick about the overheard conversation.

Approaching the rooms, he was surprised by a line of people snaking through the door and around the corner. Frowning, he pushed past the bodies and entered the workroom to find Alain with Master Barwick, both busy with clients. Alain was so engrossed in his work he did not notice him enter. Lala still slept by the fire, so John let himself into the bedroom and soon found himself drifting off to sleep.

No sooner had he closed his eyes than Alain was shaking him awake. 'Hey, how about moving over and giving me some room. I am completely done in.'

'Wha... what time is it?' he asked, bleary eyed.

'Almost time for noon meal in the great hall.'

John sat bolt upright and swung his legs over the side of the bed. 'I need to eat and prepare for guard duty.'

'Yes, you do,' Alain confirmed. 'And I need some rest if I am to attend the coronation as planned.

SWAGMAN

'By the way, Barabal called by, mumbled something about Stan having all the luck being included in the meetings today, then left instructions for us.'

Remembering how Stanislaus had been looking forward to a morning nap, he did not think the boy would consider his assignment as being lucky at all.

'Are you listening? She said to let you know you need not wait through the meal, just meet her outside the prince's bedroom. We are to relieve you before three to allow you both time to dress for this evening.'

John shook his head, trying to clear his sleep fuddled thoughts.

'Did you find out anything about the wine jug today?' he managed to ask.

'I did a test, but it was inconclusive. Although I am leaning towards some arsenic being there, I needed more wine to be certain.'

'Well, after the number of dead rats Stanislaus and I found outside a window near the prince's chambers, I think we can categorically say if he had drunk any of the wine, he would likely be dead by now.'

Alain's soft snores told him the boy had not heard a word he said. Leaving him to his rest, John opened the door to the workroom and silently closed it behind him.

In a comfortable chair by the fire, Master Barwick also slept, his mouth open and eyes closed. Lala, seeing the boy up and about, left his fireside bed on wobbly legs and walked to the door. Looking back at John, his intentions were clear.

He let the lamb out and followed him round to a grassy area at the side of the building. Walking to the other side of the lawn the lamb discretely relieved himself. On his return, the Lala started nibbling at tender shoots of grass. As his guardian ate, John told him about the meeting he had witnessed earlier in the day. Lala stopped eating.

Can you tell me the exact words Isolde used? he asked.

She said something along the lines of, "Tell me you still want the prince poisoned and I will do it", John told him.

Oh, that is close to shaping events, but I believe it is still within the boundaries. Shame. It would be easier if she had mis-stepped.

You mean you would be able to go before a judge or something, and they would tell her to stop?

John hoped the outside powers were poised to intervene, at least he would be able to stop worrying if they did.

Nothing that easy, I am afraid. How they would step in and realign events does not matter now. We need to ensure history follows the right path the old fashioned way. The lamb chewed a few more shoots of grass before looking up at John. *I guess you can let me back in now while you go and eat. Oh, and if you could bring back something for Master Barwick before you find Barabal, I am sure he would appreciate it. It is the least you could do given you slept in his bed while he took the chair.*

A couple of servants he had not seen before left the table as John arrived. They nodded hello as they departed. Left alone, he ate his meal in silence. Once he was done, he filled a plate with some cold meat, bread and cheese, then filled a cup with small beer, and took it all back for Master Barwick.

Walking back past the hall, he saw people still sitting around eating and drinking. Prince Henry appeared to be enjoying a joke with Ranulf Flambard. Isolde was nowhere to be seen. With nothing else to do, he decided he would go to the lookout early. Much to his surprise, he found Barabal sitting on the table swinging her legs and frowning.

'What is wrong?' he asked.

'You got to walk around London, Alain got to work with a renown apothecary, Stanislaus got to listen in on meetings of state. And what did I get to do? I got to sew flowers on a shirt.' She kicked her heel against the table leg, causing a resounding bang to echo around the hallway. 'Then, I had to unpick it,' she continued through gritted teeth. 'And re-sew it, because my flower was not deemed good enough for a future king.' The hall echoed with yet another bang.

'I am trusted to take letters to the future queen. I can do their dirty work for them. But as soon as I am no longer needed, I am relegated back to the sewing room.' Bang. 'It is so unfair.' Bang. Bang. BANG.

John hated to find his friend so down in the dumps, but he did not know what to tell her. His mother made similar comments over the years, and he knew over seven hundred years later, women were still not treated the same as men. All he could do was speak from the heart.

'My mother has run our farm and brought up three children without any help since my father died. And yet she is still not respected by the other local farmers because she is a woman.

'You, Barabal, are one of the most capable people I have ever met. Nothing I can say will make this right, or make you feel better. I do want you to know though, I believe you can do anything I can, and you can probably do it better. It is not fair no one recognises that, but it is the way life is.'

Barabal smiled sorrowfully. 'I know. It is so frustrating sometimes. Especially knowing that my only course of action is to marry and try and influence things through my husband. If I want to do anything at all, I need to work twice as hard as any man. Alain says I should try and affect change closer to home. Perhaps he is right.'

Barabal shrugged half-heartedly and John kept a grin in check, guessing Alain may have been thinking of a specific place close to home with a very specific person.

Outburst over, Barabal and John took turns pacing the corridor and watching the prince's room. It was not until well after one the meal in the main hall broke up. Barabal was sitting on the table dozing when Prince Henry passed and opened the door to his bed chamber.

A little while later, John nudged Barabal, and she took her turn watching the door. Worried if anything was going to happen it would be now, he slipped himself off the table and walked up and down the corridor, only to find Barabal looking concerned on his return.

'Did we miss something? Is it possible we both dozed for a moment and that girl slipped in?' Her fingers worried the fabric of her dress in agitation.

John replayed the short time since the prince returned from lunch over in his mind.

'I do not see how she could have. I think you are upset because you had a nap. Perhaps she is waiting until later, when the boys relieve us. She may think Alain and Stanislaus are easier targets.'

'Who thinks we are easy?'

The voice came from right behind John. Startled, he jumped and turned to find Stanislaus and Alain had crept up the corridor and now stood less than a few steps away from them.

'How did you do that? I did not hear footsteps,' John blurted out in surprise.

Stanislaus and Alain both held up their boots.

'We are practicing being extra quiet... and we may have taken the opportunity to play a little prank.' Alain could not wipe the cheeky grin off his face.

'And it worked.' Stanislaus' face was plastered with such a broad grin even Barabal smiled in response.

'What did you do? No, wait, do I want to know?'

'We found Tobias asleep at the back of the hall. We tied his legging ribbons together so... well, you can guess. We took our shoes off and crept out so as not to disturb him,' Stanislaus told them while putting his footwear back on.

'Have your fun while you can, boys, we will all be working until late tonight. The festivities are planned until well into the wee hours of the morning, and we have been asked to help serve and clear up.'

'Do I understand from what we overheard that Isolde did not appear this afternoon?' Alain asked.

John and Barabal shook their heads.

'Good, that means we will be the heroes again.' Stanislaus' grin grew still broader. 'So, what are you two hanging round here for, trying to steal some of our glory?' He laughed.

'We might want to stay and see how to do things properly,' Barabal teased.

A door creaked open further down the corridor and a head popped out. 'You there, keep the noise down. Mistress Barabal, what are you doing here? I am sure Robert de Beaumont would not like to find out you are cavorting with boys in the shadows.'

'No, Sir Ranulf, I am on an errand and came across these louts lounging around. I am off to the women's quarters to change for this afternoon's events now.'

Barabal feigned contriteness, but Ranulf Flambard waited until she was well down the corridor before popping his head back inside his room.

'Well, boys, keep an eye out and I will see you at the coronation.' John said as he turned to leave.

'John.' Alain stopped him. 'Master Barwick needed some sleep, so he took the bed when I woke up. You will need to be quiet. I left some proper clothes for you over the chair.'

Sighing, John looked at the boys in front of him. Both wore embroidered tunics made of fine wool over soft woollen leggings. The clothing itself was not so bad, in fact, the material was of a finer quality than their everyday clothes, as were the colours.

Alain wore a green tunic with yellow leggings, and although Stanislaus' leggings were a more sober blue, his tunic was bright red with gold trimming. Wondering what delight they had left for him, he reluctantly left them to their duties.

CHAPTER SEVENTEEN
HOW TO KILL A KING

John washed himself all over, including his hair. Now sparkling clean for the first time in days, he changed into his new clothes, which were an unassuming mix of blues and greens. He then sat down in one of the chairs, closing his eyes for a moment, or so he thought. He awoke some time later to Master Barwick trying to move around the work room without waking him. Half opening his eyes, he realised the fire had gone out and Lala had curled into his body for warmth.

'Sorry, I am afraid I do not move as stealthily as I once did.' The apothecary placed a book on the table as he offered his apology. 'I guess you are still tired from your night's vigil, the bed is free now if you want to use it.'

John's eyes flew open. 'No, thank you, master. What is the time?'

'Oh, around three, or three-thirty, I think. The high and mighty are not gathering yet, there is still time for a quick nap.'

'Thank you but my stomach is doing somersaults, I think I had better go and find out how guard duty is going.'

He pulled on his shoes and darted out the door towards Westminster Palace. The palace precinct was still awash with people all going about their business. A coronation was a big event, and preparations to ensure the day ran smoothly would continue right up until the new king went to bed.

Dashing past palace servants and guards alike, he made it to the corridor where he found Alain sitting on the table, elbows on his knees and chin in hands, and Stanislaus propped against the wall, throwing a stone in the air and catching it.

'You two are keeping busy I see,' he whispered.

Remembering they had been told off once for making noise, he did not want to risk being sent away at such a crucial time.

'Since you left, no one of note came. Nothing at all interesting happened until the prince's squire brought some bathing water and a change of clothes just before you arrived. We made him drink a little to show it was not poisoned. We thought he might be annoyed with us for asking, but he said he is used to that sort of request so prepared the water himself.'

Stanislaus sighed, stood and stretched his limbs. 'Maybe they decided against killing the prince.'

Shaking his head, John said, 'No, I am sure they will still try. Isolde would not give up that easily.'

SWAGMAN

At that moment, the door to Prince Henry's room opened and he emerged looking refreshed and energetic, and only partially dressed for his big day.

'Have you boys nothing better to do than stand around in corridors killing time?' he asked them. 'I am sure my steward can find jobs for you all.' He laughed when their faces dropped. 'Be off with you and finish getting ready for today. I understand you are all to attend my coronation. You do not want to miss a moment of it, I am sure.'

'You knew we were out here?' John's eyes widened in surprise.

'Even a deaf man would have heard the noise you made last night.' The prince seemed in high spirits. 'It is almost the hour when I will be crowned, and I am safe and well. I am sure that is in no small part thanks to you all, but you can stand down now.'

At that moment, Sir Ranulf left his room. 'And here is Ranulf come to talk with me while I dress. I will be as safe with him as I would be with you all.'

The two nobles went into Henry's bed chamber and the door closed.

'Do you think he is right? Is he safe?' Alain asked.

'For the moment, I guess. We may as well go get something to eat while we can. I am told the ceremony will be hours long and I do not want to make it seem longer by being hungry the whole time.' John led his companions away.

As they walked passed the entrance to the hall on the way to the servants dining room, Barabal accosted them.

'You left your post? Are you mad?' she hissed.

'Hold on a moment,' John told her. 'Sir Ranulf is in

with the prince, so he will be fine. If you think he needs to be babysat, why don't you go and do it yourself?'

Barabal raised her eyebrows in alarm. 'You left him with Ranulf Flambard. Are you all stupid? Much as I like the man, he was loyal to King William the Second, and with rumours going around that Prince Henry was in league with Walter Tirel planning the king's demise, he is the last person you should trust with the prince's safety.'

With that, she flounced off, leaving the bewildered boys staring after.

'She is a force of nature,' Alain commented, the tone of his voice telling them he thought that was a good thing.

'Still, does she need to make us look stupid all the time?' Stanislaus asked.

'Maybe we were a little thoughtless,' Alain said as the three boys went through the door to the dining room. 'We should take something to go, then go and help her.'

They helped themselves to some bread and cheese, not knowing when they would be allowed to eat again that day. Before they could leave, they were forced to stand aside as the servants from Winchester entered. John watched them file in and chuckled as Tobias entered carrying his ribbons, leggings pooling around his ankles. As the man glared at Alain, he could not help thinking something was amiss. Then it struck him. Isolde was not there.

Pushing past them and through the doorway, he ran from the dining room with Alain and Stanislaus close behind. Not stopping to explain, he sped down the corridor, past the guards standing sentry duty as they did when the prince was in his room, and brushing past the prince's squire and a cloaked figure, who was forced to step out of his way. As she did, he found Barabal lying in a heap on the floor.

At the very moment he recognised the girl on the ground, he realised who he had run by. Looking up, he found Isolde boldly staring back at him.

'You are too late, it is done.'

She smiled triumphantly as she turned and walked away. John was torn. He wanted to go after her, she should not be able to get away with what she had done. However, Barabal and the prince were of more pressing concern.

'John, what is it?' Alain had caught him up, followed closely by Stanislaus.

Seeing Barabal on the floor, the apprentice apothecary dropped to his knees and began checking the girl out. As he felt around her head, she stirred and opened her eyes.

'Isolde,' she said weakly. 'We must check on the prince.'

'Not yet.' Alain was suddenly in his element. 'Stanislaus, go tell Master Barwick we need an emetic.'

'A what?' Stanislaus looked confused.

'Just say these exact words: "The prince needs an emetic",' Alain ordered. 'He will understand.'

'Something to make the prince violently sick,' an exasperated Barabal told him as she sat up, now completely lucid. 'Help me to my feet, I will come with you to make sure you get it right.'

As Stanislaus helped Barabal down the corridor, Alain's gaze worriedly followed them even though she seemed as good as new. Once they were gone from sight, the boy turned to John.

'Are you ready to break into a prince's room and tell him he has been poisoned?'

Barabal sped away from the scene, dodging between nobles and servants alike, focused on her mission to bring the apothecary to the prince as fast as humanly possible.

'Do you think the prince will be all right?' She asked worriedly as she slipped around a man carrying chairs.

Stanislaus, barely able to keep up with her as it was, said nothing, saving his breath for more important things. His companion stopped dead in her tracks and swung round to face him.

'So you do not believe he will live through this?' she demanded.

Catching his breath before he answered, he finally managed a, 'I do not know. I did not get a chance to even see him before we took off.'

'Then why did you let me think... oh never mind.' Spinning on her heel she took off and the boy, still not quite sure what had just happened, had no choice but to follow after. He caught her up outside Master Barwick's rooms.

Stanislaus knocked on the door while Barabal moved from foot to foot, then up on her toes and back down. Waiting clearly was not one of her strong points. Sounds of a chair scraping across wood came from inside, and he looked around the courtyard while he waited for the apothecary to shuffle across the room and open the door.

The yard was busy, full of servants bustling around finalising preparations for the coronation, and the celebrations that would follow. He lost himself in the bustling activity until a movement by the castle caught his eye. He glimpsed a head of dark hair before the figure slipped behind a group of servants. Nudging Barabal, he pointed.

'Did you see that?'

'See what?' she asked without taking her eyes from the door.

'I think I spotted Isolde heading for the river.'

As the latch moved, Barabal turned to him. 'Well, what are you waiting for? Go after her.'

Master Barwick opened the door and glanced about in surprise as he heard the tail end of her words. Looking at Barabal, Stanislaus made sure she was not joking before he sped off through the crowd.

Unfortunately he was forced to pull up abruptly, as the cook chose that exact moment to lead a train of servants carrying tables out into the yard to be set up for the servants feast later that day. Eyes darting, Stanislaus searched for a way around the blockage. Not finding one, he ran, dropped to the ground and slid underneath a table, almost taking out the legs of one of the men carrying it. He was followed by a string of abuse as he regained his feet and took off around the edge of the castle buildings.

Pulling up short by some crates of chickens, he searched Westminster dock for any signs of his prey. She was not there but, perhaps more importantly, she was not in any of the boats leaving the castle either. That meant she was still on this side of the river.

Walking around crates and baskets containing food to feed the swelling number of nobles in London for the crowning of their new king, he made sure the serving girl had not secreted herself anywhere. Happy there was no sign of her, he considered where else she might have gone.

His roving eye caught sight of a black haired woman weaving her way along the river path against the run of the crowd. Picking up speed, he attempted to follow. However, the tall squire was not as small and nimble as the girl he chased. For every two steps he took forward, he was pushed back at least one by everyone heading to Westminster Abbey to find a spot to watch the day's proceedings.

Frustrated, he watched her move further and further away from him. In desperation, he engaged his elbows and started pushing people out of the way. He made some progress, and soon the crowd thinned enough for him to walk at a fast pace.

Just as he thought he might have a chance to catch her up, she glanced back over her shoulder and, seeing she had a tail, she slipped through the people beside her and into an alley. Overcome with panic, Stanislaus broke into a run, only to find himself flying through the air and landing flat on his face.

Turning to abuse whoever had tripped him, he found his legs tangled with a small boy wiping tears from his eyes. Overcome with guilt, he picked the lad up and handed him to his mother, apologising for his clumsiness. He received a glare in return, and he did not wait to hear the stream of angry words coming out of the woman's mouth.

By the time he made it to the alleyway, it was empty. Running to the other end, he frantically searched the street, but could see no sign of the girl who poisoned the king. Returning to the castle, head hung low, he at least consoled himself Isolde was free, but she was no longer a threat. After all, she had done what she intended to do. The only question now was whether or not she had succeeded.

John hesitated in front of the prince's door. 'What happens if we barge in and there is nothing wrong with him?' he wondered out loud, not wanting to risk another night in a dungeon.

'Here, let me.' Alain sighed and knocked firmly on the wood.

'Come,' a voice spoke from the other side.

Alain opened the door and the boys came face to face with a prince dressed in all his finery, about to take a sip from a goblet. John acted on instinct. Rushing forward, he knocked the cup from Prince Henry's hand.

The prince's face darkened, like a storm cloud blocking the sun. His jovial demeanour of the morning disappearing as he became the imperious ruler.

'Boy, you go too far. You will be hung for daring to touch your king.'

John thought about telling the prince he was not yet king, but for once held his tongue.

'Begging your pardon, sire, but we believe your wine to be poisoned.'

Alain move beside John in a gesture of support, but stopped short of laying hands on someone of royal blood.

Prince Henry frowned. 'What do you mean? My squire brought this pitcher. Anything he hands to me has already been checked by my man.'

'Think, sire, please, it is important,' Alain begged him. 'Did your page hold the pitcher of wine, or was it in Isolde's hands?'

Prince Henry's frown deepened as he tried to remember exactly what happened. 'Isolde and my squire arrived at the door at the same time. While the squire cleared my room, Isolde suggested we... ah...'

'Celebrated your coronation early?' John helped the prince out in the interests of saving time.

'Umm, yes. I told her not now, but perhaps later... Ah, she handed me a jug and said it was a pity to waste it, perhaps this would help settle my nerves. But she would not have done anything so base as to poison me. I believe she truly cares for me.

'Besides... I heard Barabal on watch in the hallway. Surely she would have—'

'She was out cold when we arrived,' Alain said. 'She had no bump on her head, so I suspect someone used a special technique to put her to sleep.'

'Oh, she is all right,' John added when the prince looked concerned. 'But I am afraid the squire must be working with Isolde.'

'He has been with me since boyhood. He would never do anything to harm me.'

'Maybe not knowingly. A pretty face can be very persuasive though. Perhaps he thought he was doing you a favour, allowing your friend some time with you in private. They did not hurt Barabal, so no harm was done. He may not even have known what Isolde was up to,' John assisted the prince again.

SWAGMAN

'I am still not convinced she did anything at all, other than try and seduce me. I feel fine.'

Alain was suddenly all professional. 'How much did you drink?'

'A few sips, perhaps half a goblet while I finished dressing. I was about to drink another when you rushed in.'

The prince gripped the bed post, swaying a little, pinpricks of sweat forming on his brow. 'Perhaps I do not feel so well after all. I had put it down to nerves. Will I die?'

'Not if I can help it,' Alain answered. 'If it is arsenic, as we suspect, all we can do is try to stop it going through your system. Can you stick your fingers down your throat and make yourself sick?'

'Really? You cannot give me something to help with that?'

'Barabal has gone to get Master Barwick. He will bring something to help empty your stomach. In the meantime the more poison we can remove now, the better your chances. Sorry, sire, I would not ask this of you, but it is for your own good.'

The prince turned away from the boys and walked over to the window. Sticking his fingers in his mouth, he made himself sick. John felt sorry for anyone walking below, but he guessed manners were not the most important thing at a time like this. A little wine came out, but not much else.

'Did you eat anything at noon time?' Alain asked.

'Yes, I was ravenous, and I did not know when I would get a chance to eat again today, so I rather over-indulged.'

'Good, that might help slow the poison's effects, but I think everything needs to come up,' Alain declared.

As the prince turned back to the window, Barabal rushed into the room clutching a vial. She shoved it towards Alain. 'Here, Master Barwick said he should drink the whole thing. And he is on his way, he shall be here presently. Can I do anything else?'

'Yes,' Alain told her, seeing her embarrassment at being in the princes's rooms. 'You can go to the kitchen and bring a large pitcher of fresh water, and another of milk.'

Barabal seemed more than pleased to do something that would take her out of the bedchamber. When she had shut the door behind her, Alain took the vial over to the prince, who was still valiantly trying to bring up his meal.

'Here, drink this, every last drop.'

Henry took the top off, and the smell had him gagging. 'I cannot.' He shuddered. 'Wait, has my man tasted it?'

'Do you want to live?' Alain was firm.

'I have been poisoned once today, I think I am right to be cautious.'

'Here,' John grabbed the vial and took a sip. 'See, I am fine.'

John swiftly handed the medicine to the prince, hoping the cramps he felt starting in his stomach was the potion doing its work rather than a sign he had been foolhardy and would die in this strange land.

Prince Henry took a deep breath, closed his eyes and downed the vial of liquid. John estimated he had no sooner finished than his stomach decided to rid itself of its contents. Henry just made it to the window before his lunch reappeared.

Wave after wave of cramps went through the prince's

body, and continued long after his stomach was empty. Exhausted, he finally slipped down the wall beneath the window, his face grey and his body shaking.

At a timid knock on the door, John opened it to find Barabal. She passed him a jug of water, and one of milk. 'It has been tasted,' she informed them before moving out of the way to allow Master Barwick entry.

'I shall be outside if you need me,' Barabal said, once again closing the door.

John laughed, for such a bossy person she had some very strange scruples about being in a man's bedroom. He turned back to find Master Barwick looming over Prince Henry. The apothecary took the pitcher of water from John and told the prince to drink it all. From the look on the prince's face, you would have thought the water was toxic, but John guessed after throwing up his breakfast, the prince's digestive system would be none too happy.

Realising his presence was no longer required, and needing to find a privy as his stomach was threatening to relieve itself of its contents, John quietly slipped outside.

Barabal sat on the floor by the door, twining her fingers through Lala's wool.

'How is he, John? Has our work all been for nothing?'

'I do not know. I am not sure if there is a cure for arsenic poisoning, but Master Barwick is doing his best, with Alain's help.' Clutching his stomach, he was about to make a run for it when he noticed someone was missing. He clenched his jaw, holding everything in as he asked, 'Where is Stanislaus?'

'He thought he saw Isolde and went chasing after her.'

As she finished speaking, the door opened and Alain emerged. 'The master will stay with the prince a while,' he informed them. 'He said from the state of him, Prince Henry probably did not ingest enough of the toxin for it to kill him outright. Thank goodness we caught him before he had that second cupful of wine. Master Barwick praised me for my quick thinking. There is a slim chance the prince will survive without any side effects. Now we just have to wait and see.'

John knew he was not going to be able to wait with them, his stomach cramped again and he took off to find somewhere to empty it in private.

CHAPTER EIGHTEEN
THE CORONATION

John and Alain waited in the apothecaries' rooms until it was time to leave for the ceremony. Master Barwick had not yet returned, and it seemed the boys would be attending the celebrations alone. The excitement of saving the prince had worn John out, not to mention the time he spent in the privy afterwards as a result of taste testing the prince's medicine. Wearily, John asked why they needed to go to the coronation at all, and immediately wished again he would learn to keep his mouth shut.

Lala decided to lecture them on being witnesses to events in history. *This is an important occasion and you have a unique chance to be at the true beginning of the devolution of royal power. You cannot miss it.*

'So, just because we can then,' Alain said as he put on his new leather shoes.

More because the new king asked you to, and you cannot give me a good reason why you should not, the lamb answered wryly.

John laughed and adjusted his clothes, then tied the yellow ribbons Alain handed him round the end of his leggings to keep them in place. Master Barwick had left them both with new leather shoes as a present, and John tried his on to find they fitted perfectly. By the time he applied the finishing touches to his outfit, he felt as trussed up as a Christmas turkey. His only consolation being Alain looked more like a peacock.

Later, sitting at the back of Westminster Abbey, John felt a lot less unhappy with his attire. Most of the common people in the back rows were dressed as he was, but when the nobility began to make their way in, he saw his clothing was plain by comparison. He wondered how the boys were not fidgeting and uncomfortable under all the jewels and fancy stitching decorating their costumes.

John's eyes widened as William of Breteuil entered the abbey, followed by the men and women of his household. Surprised the duke would show his face after what had happened, John nudged Alain so he could share the spectacle.

'He could hardly not attend, could he?' Alain muttered. 'At the moment, only our word links him to the attempted murder of the future king, and we are not yet adult and so could not be heard in a court of law. To stay away would be admitting his guilt.'

If he felt any shame at all at his actions, he did not show it as he sauntered down the aisle, head held high, taking his place in the front row along with all the others of noble birth. Some of his household were also of high enough birth to take seats in the rows behind, but a few had to make do with trying to find space at the back, or standing along the walls.

Musing how lucky he was to have been offered a seat as the wait for proceedings to start was a long one, he was distracted by Robert de Beaumont's entrance. As one of Prince Henry's closest friends, he was one of the last to arrive, and he strode quickly to his position front and centre. His household followed at a more sedate pace.

Stanislaus strode into the hall wearing a heavy tabard, sporting what John assumed must be his family coat of arms. He held out his arm, and Barabal placed a hand on it, and they followed the de Beaumont family to their seats, which were only a few rows from where the Archbishop waited to begin proceedings.

The diminutive girl looked beautiful in a finely woven blue linen dress, over top of a fine white linen under-dress. Around her waist she wore a belt of gold. Her hair fell in dark brown waves down her back, held off her face by a circlet of fresh flowers. She looked amazing. Alain obviously thought so, as he gasped in wonder as she passed their seats, giving them a cheeky wink in the process.

The church was now full to the brim, and people shuffled in their seats as the Archbishop wrung his hands, anxious for the prince to arrive. Once everyone was seated, they all waited in anticipation, and waited some more.

'Are you sure Master Barwick actually saved Prince Henry?' John asked, only to be shushed by a haughty looking woman in front of them.

Alain glared at her, daring her to say anything as he answered. 'When I left, the prince was rather grey and not looking too well, but that was two hours ago. Surely there would have been a commotion if he had taken a turn for the...'

Trumpets sounded, blotting out Alain's final words, and the prince, resplendent in his coronation robes, stood in the doorway. He made a slow procession through the gathering, and only those close to him could see how pale he was as he made is way towards the throne. Most in the room would put his pallor down to the strains of the day, but John knew better. That man was lucky to be here.

Relaxing now their job was done, John and Alain prepared themselves for a long and boring ceremony.

The proceedings may have been more exciting if he and Alain were not seated so far back in the abbey, although John suspected not. Barabal and Stanislaus were closer to the action, but the amount of times the squire turned and caught his eye, led him to believe the coronation was not particularly interesting even when you were in the thick of it.

There was a short break in the speeches as the Archbishop called for the crown and sceptre, and they were marched down the aisle. Stifling a yawn behind his hand, John studied the crowd. Many, like him, spent their time watching others rather than the ceremony. As

SWAGMAN

a few people moved in their seats, uncomfortable from hours of sitting, those standing round the edges shuffled to improve their circulation.

John's eyes pivoted back along the wall. Something caught his eye, but his brain had yet to process the information. All he knew was a deep sense of unease. There, one of the servants was inching towards the front.

Not quite sure yet whether it was anything to worry about, he attempted to stand to get a better view, only to find his tunic roughly tugged, pulling him back down in his seat.

'What are you doing, you fool? Do you want to end up back in the dungeons?' Alain whispered, drawing John's attention to the soldiers spaced around the room.

'But...'

Marshalling his thoughts without taking his eyes off the moving figure, he found the words he needed.

'Someone is moving through the crowd up the front. There is something about them, something familiar. Maybe the dark hair?'

At that precise moment Stanislaus turned, while appearing to follow the procession in the centre isle, he took the opportunity to grin at his friends. As he raised his arm to wave, John jerked his head to the side, attempting to direct the other boy's gaze to the figure now nearly at the front of the church. Just as the squire frowned quizzically, Barabal pulled his arm back down and said something, causing the boy to shrug.

Helplessly, John considered his other options as he watched Stanislaus' head bend down towards his companion. His lips and hands moved excitedly. John could only hope the boy had understood the meaning of his gesture. Ever so slowly, Barabal's head lifted and she looked towards John. He nodded towards the person slipping in and out of sight. She glared back at him.

'Oh, for goodness sake,' Alain said as he raised his arm and pointed to where John wanted the girl to look.

Barabal followed the line of his finger and he saw her jaw drop as she finally understood what worried them. In that split second John also realised why he was so concerned. Isolde had not finished with Prince Henry.

As he found the Time Wrecker again, he followed her progress as she slipped in and out of view, then finally ducked in behind the flowers decorating the alter. They had moments before she was able to strike at the prince. John did not know what to do. He was so far back in the cathedral, even if he yelled, they would not hear him at the front, and the guards would no doubt remove him before he could do anything.

He turned questioningly to Alain, only to find the boy was not there. Looking down, he found him using his smaller body to good effect, crawling underneath the pews towards the isle. While admiring his resourcefulness, John knew he would not be fast enough to stop whatever Isolde intended.

However, he need not have worried. Glancing forward, he found Barabal raising herself from her seat. Swaying slightly, she swooned gracefully to the ground. The prince rose from his throne and quickly made his way to their friend's side. At the same time Isolde emerged from behind the alter, knife raised.

The crowd gasped as Stanislaus launched himself

towards the prince's would be attacker. Staring in dismay as all eyes in the church turned to her, the girl darted past the assembled clergy. The determined squire launched himself at Isolde, managing to grasp her foot. Unfortunately he brought her to the ground just as one of the guards had been about to grasp her. The would be assassin crawled through the legs of the prince's men, and darted for the back of the church, Stanislaus in her wake.

As if unaware of what was occurring behind him, Prince Henry called for someone to assist Barabal from the church. Two guards gently escorted the girl out. Head down, she used a curtain of hair to hide her face from the gathering. Barabal's eyes widened as she reached the end of their pew and found Alain peering up at her. Stumbling a little, she raised her head slightly and grinned at John before being escorted out.

Henry returned to his throne. He must have said something to ease the situation, as people near the front tittered in nervous release. Robert de Beaumont glared at de Breteuil, while the duke studiously ignored his gaze, choosing to concentrate on the scene in front of him as the crown was lowered on Prince Henry's head, and he was finally declared king.

The sound of trumpets filled the church as Prince Henry, no, King Henry I, stood. Robert de Beaumont joined him and placed an ermine robe around his shoulders.

'Long Live King Henry.' De Beaumont raised his voice, and he was answered by the nobles of the land.

'Long live King Henry.'

Looking every bit the king he now was, the new monarch of Briton walked down the central aisle and out of the church to cheers from the crowd waiting outside. The nobility followed in his wake, creating a colourful parade out of the abbey.

John, with Alain now back by his side, slumped in his seat and congratulated himself for a job well done.

When it was finally John and Alain's turn to leave the church, the shouts of the people for their new king were still strong. The royal party paraded back to Westminster Palace for the celebrations, but many people mingled around out front, waiting for the crowds to thin before making their way to the banquet.

There was a bright spot in the day. Earlier, while they were dressing, a messenger delivered an invitation from Prince Henry, requesting the two boys join the celebratory meal in the hall. So, instead of facing a night working, they would now be able to have some fun. While they waited for Barabal and Stanislaus to join them so they might all sit together, John passed the time people watching.

Sir William de Breteuil and his followers assembled with a group of men who did not look quite as jubilant as the rest of the gathered nobility. John imagined they still could not afford to absent themselves from King Henry's celebrations, lest they be associated with such a public attempt on the prince's life.

Before Alain had left Prince Henry that afternoon, he had requested they tell no one of the attempt to poison him. If it were known someone tried to kill him, he would be forced to find and punish everyone involved. When Alain asked why that would be bad, he had answered.

'After my brother's time as king, Briton needs healing, strong leadership and a chance to refill her coffers. A witch hunt for a potential killer would drain resources, and might potentially turn baron against baron. Not the best start to my reign.

'Besides, my guess is de Breteuil took part in this, and he will be heading back to Normandie after the ceremony, no doubt to report back to my brother. So, as it stands, I will have little time to prepare before facing my true opposition, and there are more important things to do than to waste what little time I have chasing down my poisoners.'

They all agreed to keep this attempt to themselves, and for their assistance Prince Henry issued his generous invitation, adding a special note saying he would like to meet with them all after the feast.

De Breteuil turned to head to the palace and caught John's eye, then attempted to walk around the two boys as if they were not there. John, unable to help himself, stepped directly into the man's path.

'So, both your attempts to kill Prince Henry failed.'

'I have no idea what you are talking about. Out of my way.' The duke pushed past John only to come face to face with Alain.

'Running home, tail between your legs, are you? We will be well shot of you and your Norman friends.'

Haughtily raising his head, de Breteuil's tone was strangely sad. 'Perhaps I did wrong, but I did what I did because I believed it was for the best, as did you.

'Yes, you will get your Saxon Queen, and your land-holders will be given some governance over their own lands, but at what cost? Robert Curthose will not let this go. There is bound to be war, and that benefits none of us.'

The Duke strode past, and John stood statue still as the baron's words sunk in. Until de Breteuil had spoken he had felt proud of their victory, but he was having second thoughts. Now, at the very end of his mission he learnt there was no good or bad side, no true right or wrong. There were only people fighting for what they believed in. In that moment he realised he had learnt a great truth about the trouble in his own time.

'I guess you must be mighty pleased with yourself.'

John jumped as the person spoke close to his ear. He had been so engrossed in his own thoughts, he had not heard Isolde slip in behind him.

'Is it not dangerous for you to come back just to gloat?'

'The crowd is my friend today, helping me evade the guards. Their movement has brought me this opportunity to tell you, you may have won this round, but you cannot win them all. My time will come. Until we meet again, young Time Guardian.'

John swung around, searching for a guard, but there were none in sight. When he turned back, Isolde was nowhere to be seen. At that moment, Barabal and Stanislaus appeared, and John decided to forget about Time Guardians, Wreckers and politics for just one night.

CHAPTER NINETEEN
TYING UP LOOSE ENDS

Y ou did not want to consider staying and accepting King Henry's offer? LaLa asked John as the boy changed back into his own clothes, packed his pack, and attached his swag.

'Being squire to a king would be exciting, and a great honour. However, if I stayed, I would be running away from my own life. I need to go back and do what I can in my own time to make sure the changes we started here will continue. Perhaps this time I might even be able to help people see things a little differently.'

I expected nothing less from you. Your sense of responsibility is one of the reasons you were chosen to help. LaLa sounded like a proud parent.

'And maybe also because I had a lesson or two to learn here?' John smiled.

I am surprised to hear you learnt anything at all, the lamb chuckled.

'Well, I did. Perhaps to maybe think before I speak.'

And...

'All right. I give in. I also learnt there is no absolute right and wrong in any argument, although I am not sure how I can use that when I get back.'

I am confident you will find a way.

'You are going to say good-bye to Stanislaus and Barabal before you leave, aren't you?' Alain asked as they quietly left the apothecary's rooms so as not to disturb Master Barwick. He was sound asleep in a chair by the fire, having indulged a little too much during last night's festivities.

John paused, wondering if he should rethink his earlier decision to just slip away. 'I am not sure how to explain everything to them. I think it is best if I just leave.'

Those two are not yet far enough into their cycle to understand why John is here, and where he has come from. Their time will come, LaLa told them cryptically.

John stared down at the lamb. 'I guess you are not going to explain that any further?'

The lamb cocked his head to the side. *Those who help guardians on their quests develop powers and understanding over many life-times. When they are ready, they learn more about us and they are asked to assist on a mission. Barabal and Stanislaus must gather more life experience and awareness before they become assistants.*

John shook his head. 'Interesting though all that is, it is past time I returned to where I belong. How do we do this?'

SWAGMAN

Follow me.

John and Alain followed Lala out of the castle precinct and down to the banks of the Thames. In the pre-dawn morning, only a few people were about. They were so busy clearing up after the day before, they paid very little attention to two boys and a lamb.

Where do you want to go back to exactly? I am assuming not to where I found you? Home perhaps?

Thinking for a moment, John smiled. 'Not to my home, and most certainly not back to the billabong. If you can manage it, I would like to go back to the shearer's camp. I think I need to return and work with the moderates there to bring about peaceful change. Put what I learnt here to good use.'

He turned to Alain. 'Thank you for your friendship, I will not forget you.' He hugged the other boy. 'Please tell Barabal and Stanislaus I shall miss them too.'

Alain brushed a tear from his eye. 'I will never forget you either. Stay safe and well.'

Come on, you two, there is no need for long goodbyes. You are destined to meet again, although not in this lifetime. Come on John, let us be off.

Alain and John frowned and looked at Lala as the lamb walked towards the gently lapping waters of the Thames River.

'Whoa, hold on there, I am not going in that water.' John's face twisted in horror at the thought of entering the sludgy, sewer ridden river below. 'We might catch something.'

How else do you think you are going to get back? I need water to create a portal.

John swore the lamb smiled. Alain also appeared a

little sick at the thought of anyone going in the water that was London's primary sewer outlet.

'Can we at least find somewhere cleaner, further along the river perhaps?'

We would need to go some way away to find anywhere less polluted. Besides, the magic used to create the portal will protect us from anything in the water. Do you want to go or not? I am happy if you want to stay here and take up Henry's offer.

'All right, we should go.' John took a deep breath, not sure whether he was more nervous about entering the water, or going back home.

Pick me up and walk backwards, just as you did at the billabong.

Picking the lamb up, John climbed down the slimy steps and on to the muddy bank. Trying to put thoughts of the scummy Thames water lapping at his ankles out of his head, he fixed his eyes on Alain and walked backwards into the river.

The water rose against the back of his legs, and as it did the current became swifter. When it reached his knees, he was swept off his feet by the incoming tide. Shuddering at the thought of any Thames water actually getting inside him, he firmly closed his mouth and eyes. As he did, he began to feel nauseous as he fell into a swirling vortex. The world went black, and the next thing he knew he was waking up with the scorching Australian sun on his face.

You will be safe from here, thank you for your help. Until next time.

John arose on shaky legs, happy to find himself in a

familiar landscape.

'Is that it? When will we meet again?'

Suddenly reluctant to let his lamb go, John delayed the moment as long as possible.

I am afraid I must hurry back as Master Barwick and I have a very important appointment to keep, and the portal will not remain open for long. You will do well from here. I checked your future, and you have much to look forward to. Although I cannot tell you any details I can say your life will, on balance, be a happy one. Goodbye and live well John Smith.

The lamb blinked out of sight. Shrugging his bag over his shoulder, John headed down the road towards the shearer's camp, all the while thinking how much lonelier it was travelling without companions.

Whistling to keep his spirits up, he put his hands in his pockets and touched something metal. Pulling his hand back out, he found two five pound coins; more money than he had ever held at one time in his short life. It was enough for him to survive for a few months without needing to work. Things were looking up.

A little while later he turned the bend, and he was back where it all started. Although he had only been gone a short while, the tents were fewer in number, and the camp looked tired and defeated. As he drew closer, he spotted a familiar figure packing up his swag and tent.

'Bill. Bill, what has happened here?'

'Why, young John, you are just about the last person I expected to see. Have you come back to join us?'

'Ah, yes, I had a change of heart. But what happened to the camp?'

'We are being moved on. After the riots the locals no longer wanted us hanging around. Most of the others have left, there are only we few stragglers now.'

'Oh.' John's stomach sank. 'I am too late then.'

'That depends on how committed to the cause you are.' Bill stopped what he was doing and looked up. 'A few of us are heading over to Brisbane. We are thinking about joining up with the general worker's union, and seeing if we can bring about change for more than just we shearers.'

John's mood immediately lightened. 'Do you think I could come along?'

'It won't be easy, you know. They arranged places for us to stay, and promised some work on the docks, but you might be able to get by and still send a little home to your family. What I am going for though, is the promise we will be able to join their union and help them bring about some changes. I am sure they would welcome a thoughtful young man like yourself.'

'I guess I could at least come along and see what it is like,' John told him, thinking maybe this was an opportunity to make a change for the better in Australia.

'Good. Good.'

'We are ready when you are, Bill.'

John turned at the sound of a new voice, and almost fell over in shock.

'Are you all right? You look a little pale there.' The boy reached out and grabbed his arm, as if to make sure he did not collapse.

'No, no I am fine. It is just you look very much like someone I know.'

SWAGMAN

'I guess introductions are in order, since we are all to be travelling together. John, meet Stan, the local constable's son. He joined us just after you left. He did not like the way the shearer's were treated after the riot, and decided to come to Brisbane and help us make some changes for the better.'

Alain gazed at the Thames water lapping against the dock, pondering his friend's departure from London. He had watched John, carrying the lamb guardian, back slowly into the water. The river swirled around in a circle, and then they disappeared.

It was not until that moment he actually believed a talking lamb had brought a boy from the future to help make sure Prince Henry became king, and enacted his charter. Now he could not deny the evidence of his own eyes. He was unsure if Lala was coming back, not that he was waiting for him exactly, rather he was trying to decide what to do with his life from here.

Last night the newly crowned king gave them his thanks for their efforts. John had been offered a small parcel of land and a position of squire with the king, which he politely turned down, saying he thought it was time he returned home. Stanislaus agreed to join King Henry's personal guard as a captain, flushing with pride as he did.

Barabal had been a different story. At first the king offered to make her a good marriage to a kind man.

Fortunately, she managed to contain her temper, although disdain was written all over her face. In the end she settled for an expensive piece of jewellery.

Alain had been amazed she accepted the necklace until Barabal explained her decision. If the king gave her property, title would transfer to her husband on her marriage. However, her jewellery would remain her own for ever. Personal wealth for a woman was a form of independence.

The king had not offered Alain anything, he merely told him to talk with Master Barwick, and if his future was not settled after, then King Henry had some ideas of his own on how to reward the boy who saved his life.

That evening, Master Barwick had offered Alain the position of journeyman apothecary. He had no family, and in time, he would pass his practice on to Alain. The master was most persuasive, but it would mean staying in London, leaving his family and, well, he had to admit he did not like the idea of leaving Barabal.

Then there was the conversation he overheard as they waited for the king. King Henry had received a report of an outbreak of St Anthony's fire in the New Forest, affecting much of the local community. They were petitioning for aid. Through the door they heard the newly crowned king tell his friend, Robert de Beaumont, he believed the New Forest might be cursed.

Having two of his brother's die in the forest, now this, he wondered out loud if his father had been wrong to place the land under royal charter. He spoke of removing the charter and washing his hands of the whole place.

Alain considered returning home. He had long wondered

if it was something in the grain that caused the skin rashes, blisters and hallucinations of St Anthony's fire. He would welcome an opportunity to study the outbreak, and perhaps find something to cure it, or at the very least, relieve the symptoms.

Then again, if he helped with the outbreak, would King Henry still want to give the New Forest back to the people of Briton? In his opinion, the return of any land seized after the Norman conquest had to be a good idea. He thought perhaps he might even petition for restoration of the property stolen from his father.

As he mulled over his future options, he saw the water by the dock swirl and a lamb pop up. Lala walked across the water to the bank, and Alain wandered over to meet him.

Your musings can be heard a mile away.

'Well, I have a lot to think about.'

You think the New Forest should be for everyone? How would you feel if I told you it will become a national treasure to be enjoyed by all if you leave it as it is?

'And I should just take your word for that?'

Alain heard a sort of a buzz in his head, as if the lamb spoke to someone, but he could not quite catch the conversation.

Come with us. You can find out for yourself.

'Come where? With who? Oh, like John? You want me to go back in time and help you fix something.'

You are nearly right. I want you to come forward in time, and help us with a little problem Master Barwick and I need to deal with.

Alain stared at the lamb in wonder. So many things

ran through his mind, but all he said was, 'Master Barwick?'

Yes, the master has helped us before. His scientific skills will be needed on this trip, but we are able to take you along too if you want to come. You might be of help to him, and you will be able to see how you work together before deciding on his offer.

'Umm...'

You might also learn some useful skills to help you with the outbreak of St Anthony's fire.

'I have to say, that is tempting.'

We can have you back before anyone realises you left.

'Please stop reading my mind. Where and when would we be going?' Alain was not sure why he was even considering the lamb guardian's offer, but he was.

Quite some way in the future, beyond John's time. Something strange is happening in the New Forest, and we need to find out whether the trouble they are having with dogs is more than it seems on the surface. That is why I need Master Barwick's skills. At the very least, you can see what becomes of the New Forest if King Henry does not touch it.

They started walking back towards the palace.

'And you are sure you can bring me back before anyone knows I am missing?'

Of course.

Alain followed the lamb back to Master Barwick's lodgings, deep in thought. A man carrying a barrel of wine bumped into him, pulling him from his reverie.

'Sorry,' the man mumbled as Alain stepped aside to allow him past.

As he did, he glimpsed the man's face and stopped

dead in his tracks. With his dark hair and tall build, the boy looked very familiar.

'That boy looks like... Was that John?'

John? Of course not, he is back home.

'But he looks exactly like... never mind.

Well, will you come with us?

Alain paused, trying to appear to be considering the offer, but excitement wriggled in his stomach and he knew the decision was already made.

'All right, I will come.'

EPILOGUE

'That was a close call, perhaps a little too close,' Alpha admonished Beta. 'I told you we were too quick to raise Sigma to our ranks.'

Beta's life form thrummed with annoyance. This debate was not new. For some reason Alpha had taken a dislike to Beta's protege, taking every opportunity to belittle the new Time Guardian. At least this time he was doing it in private, not in front of the rest of the council.

Patiently Beta responded, 'There was no way of knowing the Time Wreckers would interfere with this little slice of history, let alone send one of their most experienced operatives. Anyway, it all turned out well in the end, with Sigma's guidance.'

'And now you want this new guardian to take a trainee and a helper into the mayhem that is twenty-first century England, to deal with perhaps one of the biggest threats

to our timeline.'

'I think you exaggerate, Alpha. They go to investigate a problem with dogs dying, to assess whether or not this is part of a bigger threat in that time period.'

'There will likely be Time Wreckers there, either working with the instigators, or observing as we are. Will Sigma really be able to handle it? Or will we have to pull them out, disrupting the timeline even more? Or worse still, losing Zeta's replacement while he is still only a trainee.'

Beta's life form darkened as he realised Alpha insinuated Sigma was not able to deal with events smallest of small problems. He had trained the boy himself, and knew he was more than capable of dealing with anything the timeline threw at him. Now, if only he would prove it to Alpha.

'We can only watch and wait. The council already approved this mission, and only they can decide to end it.'

'I will be keeping a close eye on the situation.'

I am sure you will be, Beta thought to himself as Alpha winked away.

ABOUT THIS BOOK
HOW MUCH IS FICTION
AND HOW MUCH IS REAL?

On 2 August 1100, King William Rufus, William the Second, was shot in the New Forest. His brother, Henry Beauclerc moved swiftly to seize the royal treasury from its holder, Ranulf Flambard, on the very day of the king's death. On the 6th of August, a mere four days later, Prince Henry was crowned King in Winchester Abbey. He was supported by his close friend Robert de Beaumont and opposed by his brother, Duke Robert Curthose of Normandy, who was championed by William of Breteuil.

On the 11 November Henry married Princess Matilda, sister of the King of Scotland. That month he also enacted the Charter of Liberties. Before her marriage, Princess Matilda studied at Romsey Abbey, under the guidance of her aunt, who was the abbess.

William Tirel was accused of shooting the arrow that killed King William, but this has never been proven, nor does anyone know whether the arrow to the stomach was a deliberate act or, an accident.

The political details in this book relating to Henry's manoeuvring to gain the support of the barons and church are well documented, as are relations between William the Conqueror's three sons.

In 1890 in Australia, shearers began a strike over pay and conditions. Banjo Patterson wrote the song Waltzing Matilda at the time of the Queensland shearer's strike, and this was the starting point of my story. Everything and everyone else exists only in my imagination.

Australian Country Meets Medieval England - how this all came together.

As I sat with my father in his hospital room, listening to his country music (Banjo Patterson was a favourite), and reminiscing on the stories he told us as children, an idea came to me. I started telling my father a story about how the swagman did not die in the billabong, but fell through to medieval times (dad loved the Knights of the Round Table).

Then I wove in my father (Alain), and added a character representing all of his friends (Stanislaus). Some of the antics of my father and his friends made it into this book (the cart in a ditch and blowing things up, tying shoe laces), making it truly a story for my dad.

As I wrote and researched some more, I had a feeling this book was meant to be because everything fell into place way too easily.

When the swagman left Australia in the 1890s I wanted him to fall into Medieval England to a time when the supremacy of kings began to erode. I typed in a google question, as you do, and the first thing that came up was Henry I and his Charter of Liberties. I had expected hours of trawling to find a time in history to link with the ideals of the strike, and there it was in front of me.

Serendipity then kept giving. Henry's accession to the throne came with its own dramatic plot line. The unexplained death of a king, followed by a struggle for power. It would be difficult to imagine a plot line this twisted.

To top it off, King William the Second, William Rufus, died in Hampshire's New Forest, then was taken to Winchester. Only a few months, before I had been with family visiting the New Forest. I had started planning a story that linked the past to the present set in a town we visited. (This will now be book two in the Guardians of Time Series).

The bow to wrap this gift came in the form of Henry's wife, who was coincidentally christened Princess Matilda, but more often called Edith. Amazing, as swagmen and shearers used to call their bedrolls Matilda, hence the song name Waltzing Matilda.

ABOUT THE AUTHOR

Vivienne has been writing books since she was fifteen years old, but only friends and family were allowed to read them. Forced to give up work because of family commitments she was encouraged by friends and family to finally put some of her writing out there for others to read.

In the real world after leaving university with a BA in History and Politics she worked as a Personnel Officer, an Office Manager, a Project Manager, a DBA and IT Manager then as a Business and Data Analyst, adding an MSC in Information Systems along the way. In her world she continued to write.

Born in Invercargill (New Zealand), she has lived in; Dunedin (New Zealand), London (England), Petersfield (England) and currently lives with her husband and son and their dog Trouble and kitten Lola in Sydney (Australia).

ACKNOWLEDGEMENTS

This book has been rather special to write, as so many of the characters come from my father's stories. So I would like to thank others who contributed unknowingly to parts of the characters in this story.

My father Allan gave rise to the character Alain, gifting him with an inquisitive mind and a love of practical jokes. His friendship with my uncle, Stan, was the starting point for the character Stanislaus. Although Stanislaus is a hodgepodge of many people, he inherited Stan's soft heart and his gift of the gab.

Thank you also to my mother, Barbara and her sisters; Dot, Avis and Marj. I struggled to fit the character of Barabal into Swagman, especially as women had a very limited role in medieval times. When I asked myself, how you all would deal with the constraints of the time, Barabal came into her own.

As always I had a load of help to bring this book to

you. My editor Heather Bosevski is a talented writer in her own right, and helped me develop this story beyond its bare bones. Another talented writer, Kim Last, worked her magic with the cover and set up of my books. And to my primary reader, Sam. Thank you for telling my first ending was lame, criticism can inspire creativity.

Lastly, to my lovely husband, Jim. Without your support and creative art work I would not have been able to visualise my story as clearly.

My first love is family and friends. My first equal love is books, but my second love is history. For this kiwi to be able to weave all three together in this story set in my two adoptive homes, has been a special treat. I hope you enjoy reading it as much as I enjoyed writing it.

This one is for you Dad.

For future releases and current news you can find Vivienne at **www.viviennelfraser.com.au** or on Facebook at **www.facebook.com/vivienneleefraser**